Shine Izzy Shine

ELLIE DAINES

ANDERSEN PRESS • LONDON

First published in 2015 by
Andersen Press Limited
20 Vauxhall Bridge Road
London SW1V 2SA

www.andersenpress.co.uk

2 4 6 8 10 9 7 5 3 1

British Library Cataloguing in Publication Data available.

ISBN 978 1 84939 529 8

Printed and bound in Great Britain by
CPI Group (UK) Ltd, Croydon CR0 4YY

Shine Izzy Shine

Also by Ellie Daines:

Lolly Luck

To Mum, with all my love

One

'What do you think?' said Kye, swivelling my chair back round.

I looked at my reflection, at the braids he'd plaited and tied into a bun. I smiled. 'I like it.'

'You look lovely, hun,' said Mum, really pleased. 'As always, Kye, you've done a fantastic job.'

'Well, I do like my clients to leave here looking fabulous,' he grinned.

'You should think about opening your own salon, Kye,' said Mum as she admired her own new hairstyle. Kye had put in extensions so her short brown hair was now a full and flowing mane.

'Hopefully I'll get to at some point.'

'And when that salon takes off, you can think about opening another one and soon enough you'll have your own hairdressing empire,' said Mum.

'An empire, eh? I must say I haven't thought that far ahead. But never say never, I guess.' Kye gave Mum a hug. 'Good luck for tomorrow, Rio. I hope you have a smashing wedding.'

'I will. I'm marrying the man of my dreams, remember? And I'll have my beautiful bridesmaid, Izzy, right beside me,' said Mum, putting her arm round my shoulder.

I was really looking forward to my mum's wedding. I couldn't wait for Malcolm, my mum's fiancé, to become my stepdad – I love him loads. It was going to be my first time being a bridesmaid and my first time wearing a proper pair of high heels – a gorgeous pair of gold-coloured shoes that looked like they'd been covered in a million crystals. I'd bought them a couple of weeks earlier when Mum and I went to Greenleighs, a big shopping centre on the outskirts of town. We were just about to go into Zara when I noticed them in the window of another shop. Apart from Sam Joyner, the cutest boy in Year Eight, I'd never seen anything more beautiful and

I begged my mum to buy them for me.

'Please can I get them, Mum,' I was saying to her as we both eyed the shoes in the window.

'I sometimes forget that you're not a little girl any more, Izzy,' she replied, her lips breaking into a smile. 'You're turning into a young woman. Of course I'll buy them for you. I know how special this moment is. It was special for me when I got my first pair of high heels. I just wish I could've had my mum there to share it.'

My mum was ten when my granny died of cancer and, even though it was years and years ago, she still misses her loads. I'm named after my gran. Her name was Isobel, but everyone calls me 'Izzy' for short.

It was so great to get the shoes and I was really looking forward to wearing them to the wedding, even if I did have one major problem – I couldn't actually walk in them very well. I'd tried practising round the house a few times, but I wasn't getting any better. I felt like a baby gazelle trying to walk for the first time.

Luckily, though, I had my mum to help me out, and she's an expert when it comes to walking in high heels. Together we turned the upstairs landing into our very own catwalk. I followed Mum along it, trying my best to stay upright, as she showed me how to walk. It was a lot of fun, but my mum managed to look so elegant as she walked up and down the 'catwalk' in her heels, whereas I was all ungainly, my legs bent out as I stumbled from the bathroom to my bedroom, trying my best not to trip up.

Sometimes I wish I was more like my mum, all confident and sophisticated, but sadly I'm not, I'm shy and gawky. The only thing I guess I have in common with her is that we're both very determined, and there was nothing that was going to stop me wearing my new shoes to the wedding, not even blisters on my feet.

After Mum and I had left the salon we went to a café across the road called Café Olé.

'You two look nice,' said the owner Marie, as we walked in.

She smiled brightly as we ordered two cappuccinos and two brownies. We then went and sat on one of the sofas. I've always liked Café Olé, especially as their brownies are super delicious. The café has been on the high street for years and Mum has been going there since she was a teenager. Back then the café used to do proper food, when another woman called Erica was running it. Mum said the food used to be amazing, especially their 'messy spaghetti', which she reckoned was called that 'cos you'd always end up splashing Bolognese sauce all over yourself.

Café Olé was also the place where my mum met my dad, Gavin. She said he was sitting on a table opposite and came over and asked her out. But a few months after I was born, my mum and dad broke up. Mum always says she was heartbroken when they split because she really loved him, even though he'd been seeing another woman behind her back. When I was just a couple of months old, he moved to Spain with that woman and my mum never saw him again.

Even though I was too young when my dad left to remember him, there was a time when I used to wish that he'd get in touch so I could finally meet him. All I have of my dad is a few photos that my mum kept so I'd know what he looked like. But it doesn't bother me that he was never part of my life because I have Malcolm who I love to bits.

Malcolm and my mum have been going out for five years, and a year ago they got engaged after we all moved into a new house. Our house is really nice and my bedroom's much bigger than my room in mine and Mum's old flat. We also have a garden that has an apple tree and a little vegetable patch where Mum grows carrots and other veg.

'I do hope Malcolm remembers to wear a pair of black socks tomorrow,' said Mum, as Marie brought over our cappuccinos and brownies. 'But being Malcolm, he'll probably wear one black sock and one yellow sock.'

'At least he won't be wearing one of his zany T-shirts,' I said, biting into my brownie.

'True. I could only imagine the look of horror on your grandad's face if he turned up in a T-shirt saying "Don't worry, be a hippy".'

Although Malcolm's brilliant, he's a total geek. He has loads of T-shirts that have wacky slogans on them. The silliest one he's got is a T-shirt that says "I'm the coolest cat in Catland", whatever that's supposed to mean. He also can't cook to save his life and, whenever he does, it'll be something that has odd ingredients in it, like macaroni cheese with peanut butter, or a chicken curry with rhubarb. It'll always taste gross to everyone except Malcolm.

'I really hope the wedding goes perfectly,' said

Mum, tapping the side of her cup.

She took out her Blackberry, and I knew that she was going to look at her weather app. She'd been checking it constantly over the last couple of days.

'The forecast still reckons it's going to be sunny, so fingers crossed.'

'Tomorrow is going to be perfect, Mum. And even if it does rain, everyone's still gonna have an amazing time,' I tried to reassure her.

'I know, I'm just worrying for nothing. You're right, it will be perfect.' She squeezed my hand gently. 'You do know you'll still be my number one person, don't you?'

I nodded.

'Me marrying Malcolm won't ever change that. We'll still get to do all the things we do now like our girlie shopping trips and getting our nails done.'

'And our hair done, don't forget that,' I added.

'Yep, we'll still go and see Kye together.'

'And what about doing karaoke together the next time we go on holiday?'

'Yep, we'll still do that as well,' she said with a giggle.

We both love to sing, Mum and me. Nearly everyone in my family has told me I have an amazing voice. It's my dream to become a famous pop star when I'm older. At my best friend Layla's birthday party, in a few weeks' time, we are planning to do a song with our two other friends, Holly and Alice. We're going to dress up as our favourite band Little Mix and sing their song 'Wings'. We'd had one rehearsal so far, practising both the song and the dance routine to go with it.

'Tell you what,' said Mum, 'when I'm back from my honeymoon, why don't the two us spend an afternoon in Greenleighs and find you something nice to wear to Layla's party?'

'Yeah, that would be great,' I replied.

'Good. Although it's a shame we won't be able to take Auntie Rhona with us. She'd love Greenleighs.'

'I can't wait to see her,' I said.

'Her flight gets in at ten tonight. Your grandad's going to pick her up from the airport. I just really hope she likes her bridesmaid dress in real life.'

'She will, I definitely love mine.'

Auntie Rhona isn't really my auntie. She's Mum's best friend and they've known each other since nursery school. They were both born on the same day, at the same hospital and, spookily, practically at the same time. Auntie Rhona lives in America now and has been there for eight years. She's an interior designer which means she helps people to make over their houses. Her own house is gorgeous. It's in San Diego in California and it has loads of bedrooms, even though it's just Auntie Rhona and her dog Tofu living there. She even has a swimming pool in her garden.

'I'm so pleased that we're finally going to be a proper family – just me, you and Malcolm,' said Mum suddenly, her eyes filling with tears.

I quickly dug around my jacket pocket and pulled out a tissue – she was getting seriously emotional in the run-up to her wedding.

'Here,' I said, giving it to her.

'You're the best daughter any mother could have. I love you so much, Izzy,' she said all soppily, wiping her eyes.

'I love you too, Mum.' I reached out and gave her a hug.

Two

'Ooh, look at you two with your new hairstyles,' said Grandad when me and Mum got home.

He gave us a kiss on the cheek as we took off our jackets. My grandad lives a couple of streets away, but in the week running up to the wedding, he'd been staying with us to help Mum and Malcolm out with the preparations. It'd been fun having him around and listening to the stories he'd always tell about when he was a young man growing up in Brazil. He'd tell me about how he used to help his dad run his grocery shop, but then, when he'd turned twenty-one, Grandad had decided he wanted adventure, so he moved to the UK. It was the sixties and he could speak hardly any English when he came, but he managed to find himself a job in a florist and years later, when the owner decided to sell the business, Grandad took it over.

He met my gran at a party he went to at a place where people have dinner then a dance (that's how he described it anyway) and he's always said it was love at first sight. I know he misses Gran just as much as my mum misses her, and in his wallet he carries a photo of him and Gran together. It's such a sweet photo, they look so in love. Grandad looks quite different now; his dark black hair has gone completely grey, along with his beard, and today he wears glasses. But even though he's older now, my grandad is still very competitive, especially when playing Scrabble, which I've never been able to beat him at.

'You have a visitor, by the way,' said Grandad, pointing towards the closed living-room door.

'That's nice. Who is it?' smiled Mum, glancing at the door.

'Oh, just someone you've been dying to see,' he winked and opened the door to reveal Auntie Rhona.

'Surprise!' she shrieked, wrapping her arms round Mum.

'Rhona! Oh, my gosh, you're here!' she squealed. 'I thought your plane wasn't getting in until tonight.'

'I thought it'd be nice to surprise you, so I got an earlier flight,' she said as she hugged me. 'Haven't you grown, Izzy! You're nearly as tall as your mum. The last time I saw you, you were only a wee little thing.'

'You do see me when we chat on Skype.'

'That's hardly the same thing, Izzy,' said Mum. 'The last time we were all together, you were only nine.'

'Which means you need to come and visit me more often,' said Auntie Rhona, folding her arms and pretending to look cross. 'Tofu would certainly love to see you again.'

Tofu was just a puppy when me and Mum went to stay with Auntie Rhona in America. Tofu's a Labrador and is one of the sweetest dogs you could ever meet. I'd love to have my own dog, but, annoyingly, I'm allergic to them as well as cats and hamsters and rabbits and grass pollen and tree pollen. I'm allergic to chicken liver pâté too, which is the allergy I'm the least bothered about as it tastes disgusting and makes me come out in a rash. Dogs, on the other hand, don't give me rashes, but they do make me sneeze like mad whenever I go near them.

'So who's looking after Tofu while you're here?' asked Mum.

'My assistant, Melissa,' replied Auntie Rhona. 'I must say, you have a really lovely house, Rio.'

'Thanks. Me and Malcolm and Izzy decorated it ourselves,' said Mum. The four of us sat down on the sofa.

'And when do I get to meet the marvellous Malcolm?'

'You're going to have to wait until tomorrow, I'm afraid. He's staying at his best man's tonight,' said Mum. 'Obviously, I wouldn't want him to see me in my dress before the wedding. I don't want any bad luck.'

'Who'd have thought, eh, two wild teenagers growing up into successful, glamorous women,' said Auntie Rhona, nudging Mum.

'Wild? I wasn't a wild teenager,' said Mum, suddenly looking a bit embarrassed.

'If you say so, Rio.' Auntie Rhona nudged Mum again and winked.

I looked at the two of them curiously.

Was there something I didn't know about my mum?

My mum had always made out that she was very sensible when she was young, even more sensible than me. She was never ever late with her homework, like I often am; nor would she stay up really late on a school night, like my best friend Layla always does; and she wasn't boy mad, like my other friend Alice. Her first boyfriend was my dad, who she met when she was twenty.

'Hey, Rio, do you remember when we used to go into Mr Preston's corner shop and would spend ages looking through the bridal magazines trying to decide which dress we'd want for our weddings one day?' asked Auntie Rhona, which made Mum smile.

'They'll be chatting about the old days all night,' whispered Grandad in my ear.

And he wasn't wrong because the 'old days' were all Mum and Auntie Rhona wanted to talk about. Grandad wasn't keen on hearing them natter on, so after dinner he went upstairs to listen to the radio in the spare room. But I didn't mind listening so I stayed in the kitchen with Mum and Auntie Rhona.

'We were going to call ourselves the Mystery

Girls,' said Auntie Rhona to me, referring to her and Mum's girl group. 'It was Julie, the other girl in the group, who came up with the name, but me and your mum never liked it. And seeing as tie-dye fashion was really popular in the nineties, we ended up calling ourselves the Tie-Dye Girls.'

My mum and Auntie Rhona never found fame, but they did do lots of mini concerts for their friends at school during break and they wrote their own songs. But my mum still loves singing even though she never got to do it professionally. She sings all the time around the house and she always loves to take part in the karaoke nights at hotels we stay at when we're on holiday.

'Do you remember that music video we did, Rhona?' said Mum.

'How could I forget,' said Auntie Rhona, rolling her eyes before looking over at me. 'Julie's brother did the video, but because Julie was so obsessed with being the centre of attention, there were lots of shots of her and hardly any of us. Me and your mum were furious.' She looked back at Mum. 'Do you remember the party that friend of Julie's brother threw? I think his name was Adam, and we both snuck out to go to it.'

'I don't remember sneaking out to a party,' said Mum, going red in the face.

'You must do. For practically a whole month we spoke about nothing else. We were sixteen and neither of us got home until about five o'clock in the morning. And don't you remember at the party, how you were singing and dancing on the table?'

'I was not!' said Mum, looking at Auntie Rhona pointedly. 'I don't even remember going to a party. I would have been too busy revising or reading a good book. Don't listen to your Auntie Rhona, Izzy, I was never that crazy as a teenager!'

Auntie Rhona raised her eyebrows.

'I guess I must have been thinking of someone else then, Rio . . . But it was fun being in a girl group, wasn't it? It's just a shame we didn't get to be real pop stars.'

Mum nodded. 'I don't think either of us were really cut out to be pop stars,' she said. 'Our voices weren't good enough, not like Izzy's.'

'I suppose you're right,' answered Auntie Rhona. 'But at least we did get to meet Kenny Kennedy!'

I already knew the story of my mum meeting the singer Kenny Kennedy. Auntie Rhona was his biggest fan. They'd snuck backstage at one of his concerts and managed to get right into his dressing room without being spotted. But just as Auntie Rhona was about to nick one of Kenny's towels, he walked in along with two security guards. Luckily they didn't get into trouble. My mum says Kenny was really nice and he even let Auntie Rhona keep his sweaty, smelly towel which he signed 'To Rhona, lots of love, Kenny'.

'We sang that song to him, didn't we? The one we wrote, oh, what was it called again . . .?' said Mum.

'It was "My Heart Melts for You",' replied Auntie Rhona with a dreamy look in her eyes. 'I used to really love Kenny Kennedy. He was drop-dead gorgeous. I tell you, if he was still singing, I'd snap up his album tomorrow.'

'Would you? 'Cos I don't remember his songs being any good, and he was all right looking, but nothing special,' said Mum.

Auntie Rhona looked a bit surprised.

'Mum, if you had a chance to be a teenager again, would you?' I asked her, but she immediately shook her head.

'I enjoyed growing up in the nineties, but there's no way I'd ever want to go back to being a teenager nowadays. I'd simply miss you and Malcolm too much.'

She kissed me on the forehead as she got up from the table. 'Right, I know it's only nine o'clock, but I fancy getting an early night. I'd hate there to be bags under my eyes in any of the wedding photos.' She gave me and Auntie Rhona a cuddle. 'Good night my lovelies. I'll see you in the morning. I hope the couch is OK, Rhona.'

'Night night, Mum,' I said.

'See you tomorrow, hun,' said Auntie Rhona. 'And don't worry. I'll be fine down here.'

Once Mum had gone up, I asked Auntie Rhona, 'Can I tell you something?'

'Sure, what's up?'

'I've got a surprise for Mum and Malcolm. Grandad knows. I'm going to sing a song for their first dance.'

'Oh, how lovely!' said Auntie Rhona. 'Gosh, I can't tell you how excited I am about the wedding, but I expect you're even more excited.'

I grinned. 'I am. Tomorrow's going to be totally amazing.'

Three

'Happy wedding day!' said me and Grandad when Mum came down for breakfast the next day.

'Aw, thank you,' she beamed. She joined us at the kitchen table and admired the food that we'd laid out.

Grandad and I had made American pancakes with crispy bacon, scrambled eggs and maple syrup, and Grandad had done his 'special hot chocolate', which is hot chocolate with a dash of nutmeg and cinnamon to make it extra delicious.

'So, how are you feeling, Rio?' asked Grandad.

'Happy, excited, and I can't wait to see Malcolm.'

She paused for a moment. 'I also can't help wishing that Mum was here,' she added, her voice faltering as she mentioned Gran.

'She will be here sweetheart, in spirit,' said Grandad. 'She loved you so much, Rio. You were always her special little girl.'

'I know,' said Mum softly.

'So what time is the make-up artist coming?' I asked Mum as she began tucking into the pancakes.

'Eleven o'clock.'

'And the limo should be here at twelve to take us to the church,' said Grandad.

'Morning,' Auntie Rhona yawned, wandering into the kitchen. She went straight up to Mum, putting her arm round her. 'And how is the bride-to-be doing on this fine, sunny day?'

'Good, thank you,' Mum said with a smile.

'Do you have lots of butterflies in your stomach?' asked Auntie Rhona.

'Yeah, thousands!' said Mum.

'Every bride feels nervous on her wedding day, but you've got us three to help you stay as relaxed and as calm as possible,' said Auntie Rhona. She took something out of the pocket of her dressing gown. 'I wanted to give you this. It's your "something blue" and "something new", Rio.'

It was a sparkly blue hair clip.

'It's lovely, Rhona, thank you,' said Mum happily.

'I'm glad you like it.' Auntie Rhona squeezed Mum's hand as she sat down at the table. 'Now, who made these scrumptious-looking pancakes?'

'Me and Grandad did,' I said. 'Try some.'

'I will. I'm feeling quite hungry and a bit jet lagged on top of that. But don't worry, Rio, I won't be dropping off to sleep as I walk down the aisle.'

'And make sure you also try some of my dad's tasty hot chocolate,' said Mum. The phone rang in the hall. She quickly got up to get it.

'So what song are you planning to sing tonight, Izzy?' whispered Auntie Rhona as she helped herself to some breakfast.

'"What a Wonderful World" by Louis Armstrong,' I told her.

It was a song that Mum loved, as my gran used to sing it to her when she was a child.

'Oh, your mum will love that. The song has always been one of her favourites,' said Auntie Rhona.

'That's why I'm a bit nervous about singing it,' I said slowly. 'I'm scared I might muck it up.'

'You won't, sweetheart, you'll sing it beautifully,' said Grandad, 'and I know you'll make your mum and Malcolm very proud. So just remember to go out there and shine, Izzy; shine and you'll have the whole audience mesmerised.'

'Bad news, I'm afraid,' said Mum, coming back into the kitchen. 'That was Camille, the make-up artist. She's had to cancel. Apparently her bathroom's flooded and she's waiting for a plumber to come and sort it, so she's not going to be able to do our make-up.'

'That's a shame,' I said, a little disappointed.

I'd been quite looking forward to Camille doing my make-up, especially as Mum said she used to do the make-up for models at fashion shows in London and New York.

'I had a funny feeling something was going to go wrong today,' said Mum, sighing, 'and now I feel really stressed.'

'Hey, there's no need to panic,' said Auntie Rhona, getting up and putting her arm round Mum again. 'I'll do our make-up. I might not be a professional make-up artist, but trust me, once I've finished with you, you'll look like a Hollywood movie star. Chin up, Rio, we've got a wedding to get to.'

'Thanks, Rhona,' said Mum, her lips curling into a smile.

After breakfast it was time for us to get ready. First Auntie Rhona did my make-up. She covered my eyelids in a light brown eye shadow and coated my eyelashes in mascara. She applied a little blusher to my cheeks and popped some pink lip gloss on my lips.

'You look very pretty,' said Mum as Auntie Rhona began to do her make-up.

I put on my bridesmaid dress, which was a burgundy colour with a gold sash in the middle. Auntie Rhona's bridesmaid dress was the same colour but hers was strapless.

When Auntie Rhona had finished doing Mum's make-up, Mum really did look a movie star.

'I can't believe that's me!' she kept saying as she looked in the mirror. 'I look so different. I can't thank you enough, Rhona.'

'I told you I'd make you look amazing,' said Auntie Rhona. 'And now I think it's time for your dress.'

Both Auntie Rhona and I helped Mum get into her wedding dress. It was a cream dress with a lace bodice and a big sweeping skirt embroidered with beads. Mum looked stunning.

'You look amazing, Mum,' I said, hugging her.

Mum put on her white satin high heels with a glittery silver bow at the back. They were very high, even for Mum.

'So what shoes are you wearing, Izzy?' Auntie Rhona asked.

'I'll show you.' I quickly went to fetch them from my room. Then I sat on my mum's bed to put them on.

'They're gorgeous,' said Auntie Rhona, impressed.

'I know. I love them but I've been having a bit of trouble walking in them.'

I stepped slowly towards the full-length mirror on the wall, my feet wobbling a little as I walked.

'You don't have to wear them, Izzy, if they're uncomfortable,' said Mum. 'Although I think all your practice has paid off and you're looking so much more confident, I still wouldn't want you to have an accident. Maybe it would be better if you wore a pair of your pumps.'

I blinked at her. There was no way I was going to wear another pair of shoes. Sometimes I really wished my mum wasn't so overprotective.

'I'm not a little kid any more, Mum. I'll be fine, honest. I'll just try to walk carefully.'

'I know you're not a little kid, Izzy, but you're the only daughter I've got so I have to keep looking out for you. I love you more than you'll ever know,' she said, pinching my cheek like I *was* a little kid. Then she sighed. 'Oh, all right, you can wear them, but *please* be careful.'

'Can I come in?' Grandad's voice suddenly boomed from behind the door.

'Yeah, come in, Dad,' said Mum, as he ambled in holding a small paper bag.

'My, my, don't you look a picture,' Grandad said, gazing at Mum lovingly.

'Do you think Malcolm will like my dress, Dad?' said Mum as she gave him a cuddle.

'Of course he will, sweetheart. You look magnificent. By the way, I have a gift for you.'

He took out a gold bracelet from the paper bag. 'I know you already have your "something blue" and your "something new" from Rhona, but here's your "something old". It belonged to your mum. She wore it on our wedding day and I know she would've wanted you to wear it at yours.'

'It's beautiful, Dad,' Mum gushed as Grandad put it around her wrist. 'I think I'm gonna cry.'

'No, don't cry!' I said. 'Your make-up will run.'

Mum nodded. 'I'll try not to, but it's not going to be easy today, especially when Malcolm and I say our vows.'

'That's why I'll be bringing these,' said Auntie Rhona, holding up a big box of tissues.

'It'll probably be me who'll be doing all the crying today,' said Grandad, his voice full of emotion. 'But then again I've always been a big softie when it comes to my Rio,' he added, as Mum leaned her head against his shoulder.

'So, now you have your "something old", your "something blue" and your "something new". You just need your "something borrowed", if you're going to abide by the proper wedding tradition,' said Auntie Rhona to Mum.

'Oh, I know what you can have as your "something borrowed". I'll go and get it in a minute,' I said to Mum as I thought of my key ring. It had a squidgy red heart attached to it, which would be the perfect gift for Mum, seeing as today was such a romantic day. It was in my jacket pocket on the coat stand downstairs.

'Right, I'm going to go back down and iron my waistcoat. I don't want any creases in it when I'm walking Rio up the aisle,' said Grandad.

'I want us to take a photo,' said Mum after Grandad had gone downstairs. 'I want to remember this moment, just me and my bridesmaids. Izzy, can you grab my mobile, please?'

'Sure,' I said, picking it up from her bedside table.

We all squeezed in together as Mum held up her phone.

'Say cheese.'

'Cheeeeese,' we smiled as Mum took a selfie.

'Luv-ley,' said Mum cheerfully.

'I want to take a photo as well,' I said, picking up my own phone from the bed. I held it out as we all said cheese again, then checked my phone to see how it came out. We looked fabulous, especially Mum. Hopefully one day I'd be a beautiful bride just like her.

'I was really worried something would go wrong today and when Camille said she couldn't come I thought, *Yep, I'm right*,' said Mum. 'But now, I don't think there's anything that can spoil what I know is going to be a perfect day.'

I went downstairs to get a drink. Grandad had the radio blaring in the kitchen as he ironed his waistcoat. He was listening to sixties music and was humming away to the song that was playing. I took out a carton of orange juice from the fridge and poured some into a glass.

'I've been practising my father-of-the-bride speech,' he told me. 'And I have to admit, I'm feeling a little anxious.'

'You'll be great, Grandad,' I said as I sat down at the table with my orange juice. 'Before your speech, just take in a couple of deep breaths which will clear your airways and help you relax. My music teacher Miss Kerrigan told me that.'

'Well, that sounds like a good tip, I'll try to remember. And I also have to try my best not to embarrass your mum. I'm sure she won't want Malcolm to know how she once dyed her hair blue.'

'What? Mum dyed her hair blue!' I said, stunned by his revelation.

Maybe Mum had been a wild teenager after all.

'Oh dear,' said Grandad, covering his mouth. 'I've said too much already.'

'Why did she dye her hair blue?' I asked him, trying to picture my mum with hair that colour, but the image I came up with made her look bizarre and nothing like Mum at all.

'It was just her being a bit rebellious,' he replied hastily. 'But I made her wash it out straightaway because I'm sure her teachers wouldn't have allowed her through the school gates with her hair that colour.' He unplugged the iron and put his waistcoat back on. 'How do I look?'

'Very smart, Grandad, very smart,' I said, giving him a small grin, but inside I was still trying to get my head around the fact that Mum once had blue hair.

'I'd better go and give Mum her borrowed gift,' I told him, getting up from the table.

'And what is the gift?' asked Grandad.

'My key ring.'

A scream suddenly came from the hall followed by a crashing sound. I looked at Grandad in a panic; his eyes were wide with alarm. We both rushed out of the kitchen and I screamed.

Lying at the bottom of the stairs was my mum, blood dribbling down the side of her face.

Four

'She's fallen, Grandad! Mum's fallen down the stairs!' I cried as Auntie Rhona came running down. 'She's not moving!'

'Rio!' Grandad shrieked.

I thought I screamed again. But the screaming was all in my head. My mouth wasn't making a single sound.

'Rio, can you hear me?' said Auntie Rhona, kneeling beside Mum and leaning her ear above Mum's face. 'She's still breathing,' she muttered. 'Izzy, can you get me the phone?'

I wanted to get the phone. I wanted to do all that

I could to help my mum but I was too shocked to move.

'Here, use mine,' said Grandad, taking his mobile out of his pocket, but it was as if he was saying it in the distance; both his and Auntie Rhona's voices sounded like echoes around me.

Please be OK, Mum, I thought as Auntie Rhona called for an ambulance.

She must have tripped – her left shoe was partly off her foot.

'Don't worry, Izzy, your mum's going to be OK,' said Grandad in Portuguese but his face was full of fear.

Still, I couldn't answer him; it was like I'd lost my voice. I turned and staggered up the stairs. I went into Mum and Malcolm's bedroom and pulled down a shawl that was hanging on the hook on the door. I was doing it all in a daze, but it was as if there was a voice in my head telling me that I needed to keep Mum warm. I'd seen people do a similar thing on *Casualty*. My black pumps were on the landing. I kicked off my heels and slipped my feet into them, then went back down. Grandad was now kneeling beside Mum while Auntie Rhona stood looking on, her face completely stricken.

I carefully put the shawl over Mum.

'Malcolm, I should call Malcolm,' I mumbled, finding my voice again.

'Yes, he'll need to know,' said Auntie Rhona shakily, handing me Grandad's mobile.

Even though I knew Malcolm's number, I suddenly couldn't remember it. I couldn't think. Luckily his number was in Grandad's contacts.

'Julius, hello!' said Malcolm, picking up the phone. There was a lot of noise in the background and I didn't know what to say. I looked down at Mum as Grandad and Auntie Rhona carefully put her into the recovery position. She looked so fragile.

'Are you all set, Dad?' Malcolm continued. 'I guess I can start calling you that, seeing as I'm about to become your son-in-law.' He laughed. 'Me and Vince are in the pub. Don't worry, we're not getting drunk. Well, I'm not. Vince thought I needed a bit of Dutch courage so we're having a quick pint before we walk over to the church. How's Rio? I bet she's looking beautiful.'

I gulped. 'It's me, Malcolm.'

'Izzy, oh, I thought—'

'It's Mum.'

I didn't know what to say next. I didn't know how to break such sad news on a day that was supposed to be the happiest of Malcolm's life. But he'd already sensed the worry in my voice.

'Has something happened?'

'My mum, she's . . .' I closed my eyes and took a deep breath. 'She's had an accident . . . she fell. She's unconscious. We're waiting for an ambulance.'

'Oh gosh, Izzy . . . Where did this happen? How did she fall?'

'She fell down the stairs. I think she might've tripped.'

'Fell down the stairs! Oh my god,' he murmured, breathing rapidly. 'Right, I'll head straight to the hospital. I'll see you in a bit.'

'What did he say?' said Auntie Rhona.

'He's gonna meet us at the hospital.' I looked down at Mum again. It was like I was in a terrible nightmare.

The ambulance came quickly. They wanted to know Mum's name and, as they started checking her over, they were talking to her as though she were wide awake.

'She will be OK, won't she?' asked Grandad as they lifted Mum onto a stretcher.

'We'll know more when we get her to the hospital,' said one of the paramedics.

As they wheeled Mum out of the house, a white limo pulled up on the other side of the road. It was supposed to take us to the church, but now it would be taking me and Grandad to the hospital. Grandad helped me put on my jacket, just like he used to when I was little, but I didn't mind because it kind of made me feel safe. He took my hand as we walked out.

Auntie Rhona went in the ambulance with Mum and we followed in the limo. When the limo reached the hospital, through the tinted windows I could see a couple of people looking our way. They had their mobile phones held up like they were about to take a photo, but when Grandad and I stepped out they all put their phones back down. I guess they'd thought it would be someone famous come to visit some sick children or open a new ward. I doubt they were expecting a distraught girl in a bridesmaid's dress and a frightened old man.

Auntie Rhona was waiting for us in the hospital lobby with a nurse.

'Where have they taken my daughter?' Grandad asked her instantly.

'She's been taken to the trauma unit. The doctors will want to carry out a brain scan and some other tests to find out how severe her head injury is,' the nurse replied. She then ushered us into a side room and asked Grandad and Auntie Rhona lots of questions, like had Mum been drinking alcohol before her accident, or had she taken any illegal drugs. They told her that she hadn't. But all I wanted to know was when I could see her. I asked the nurse, but she said we would have to wait until the doctors had run their tests.

'She's still going to get married,' I told Grandad and Auntie Rhona as we sat in the room. 'She's going to wake up and we're all going to go to the church and then the reception. It's still going to be a perfect day, just like Mum said.'

I'm sure I must have sounded crazy, but I had to stay positive for Mum's sake. I took my keys out of my jacket pocket and squeezed the red heart on the key ring. I silently made a wish for my mum to wake up, as though the key ring was a lucky charm. I had to believe that she'd be all right, I just had to. That feeling filled my mind, pushing out a very scary thought that was trying to invade it.

'I don't think there is going to be a wedding today, sweetie,' said Auntie Rhona. 'But I'm sure as soon as your mum is better, the wedding will be rearranged and she'll still get to have her perfect day.'

'No, there will be a wedding and Mum's gonna be fine,' I insisted, but deep down I knew Auntie Rhona was right.

A short while later Malcolm arrived with his best man Vince. I ran into his arms as he gave me a huge, comforting hug.

'How is she?' he asked.

'The doctors are carrying out tests. I'm so scared, Malcolm,' I whimpered.

'Don't be. Like I said on the phone, I'm sure she'll be OK,' he said, kissing me on the forehead.

'Yeah, I'm sure your mum will be A-OK,' said Vince, slurring his words.

He was drunk and I suddenly found myself feeling really cross. How dare he be drunk on my mum's wedding day? No doubt he would've embarrassed her and Malcolm at the church. I just hoped he hadn't lost my mum's ring which he was carrying as part of his best-man duties.

Grandad looked just as furious.

'Maybe you should go and get a coffee, mate, sober up,' said Malcolm and quickly handed Vince some change. 'I'm sure they have a canteen somewhere.'

'All right, mate. I'll see you later,' Vince burbled, patting Malcolm on the back.

I definitely hoped we wouldn't be seeing him later.

'So, have they said anything else about Rio's condition?' asked Malcolm desperately, his face anxious.

'They're not telling us anything at the moment,' said Auntie Rhona. She gave Malcolm a hug too. 'I'm sorry that we're meeting for the first time under such sad circumstances,' she murmured, and that's when I started to cry.

Malcolm sat down and put his arm round my shoulder. He took out the burgundy handkerchief from the breast pocket of his smart suit and gave it to me.

I wiped my eyes then blew my nose in it hard.

'Oh no, I've spoilt your hanky now. You won't be able to wear it,' I said, feeling guilty.

'Don't worry about it. You can hold onto the hanky if you want,' he whispered. 'Tell me what happened, Izzy.'

'I think she cracked her head, Malcolm . . . it was bleeding. I'm scared she's gonna . . .' I couldn't bring myself to say the word. I slammed my eyes shut, trying to make that word disappear but it continued to scream loudly inside my head. But Malcolm knew what I meant.

'She's not going to die,' he said firmly. 'Rio's strong, Izzy, she'll pull through.'

'He's right, sweetheart, she will pull through and she'll be her same old self again when she does,' said Grandad, smiling, but I'd never seen his eyes look more sad.

Grandad stepped outside the room to make a few phone calls, walking up and down outside the door as he called his nephew Kevin, who was waiting at the church with all the other guests. He told Kevin about the accident and said he should let everyone know that the wedding was cancelled. He phoned the hotel that was hosting the reception to let them know that we wouldn't be coming. And he called Belinda, Kevin's sister, who had made the wedding cake and told her to take it back home. Malcolm rang the DJ he'd booked for the evening to tell him he was no longer needed. The DJ sent his love and sympathies as did everyone else. Malcolm got a call from Vince, who was now a bit more sober and was planning to get a taxi home. He sent his love and an apology for being sloshed. My best friend Layla, who I'd invited to the wedding, sent me a text.

Heard about yr mum. So soz.
Hope ure okay. Layla xoxo

I texted her back.

Thanx Layla. Iz xoxo

It felt like days were passing as we waited to get an update on Mum. And it was as if the nurses didn't want to tell us anything, it was like they wanted to keep Mum's condition a big secret that only they knew about. All they kept saying was: 'We need to run more tests.' And they still wouldn't let us see her.

'Are you hungry? Would you like me to get you something to eat?' Malcolm asked me.

'No, I'm OK.' It was nearly five o'clock. None of us had eaten a thing since breakfast. But I didn't feel like eating. My stomach was throbbing with pain like it had a pile of rocks in it, all knocking about.

'What about you, Julius? Do you want something to eat?' Malcolm asked Grandad.

'Answers are what I want,' said Grandad. He was beginning to look really stressed. 'I need to know what's wrong with my daughter.'

'I'll go and find out what's happening,' said Malcolm calmly, getting up from his chair. 'I'm sure one of the doctors will be able to tell us something.'

He left the room. A couple of minutes later he returned with sandwiches.

'I know you said you weren't feeling hungry, but I thought I'd get you this in case you start feeling a bit peckish,' he said, handing me a sandwich. 'It's your favourite, cheese and tomato.'

'I thought you went to find a doctor,' said Grandad, looking disappointed. He didn't seem interested in his sandwich and put it down on the floor. I did the same.

'The doctor who I need to speak to is with Rio at the moment,' said Malcolm.

Another hour passed, but we still had no further news on Mum and I was starting to get seriously fed up. On top of this, Grandad kept getting up and sitting down over and over, which had begun to annoy me. It was like he was allergic to his chair.

But he wasn't the only thing that was irritating me, everything was: the clock ticking above our head; the intermittent drone of ambulance sirens outside; the noise from the corridor – nurses chatting, a mop splashing, trolleys rattling, people sobbing, patients howling, and a man who couldn't stop coughing. It was all too much; I felt like just getting up and going home. But then I also didn't want to miss the moment when they'd say we could see Mum. So I knew I had to stay.

At seven o'clock a doctor finally came in and we all stood up promptly as if he were a member of the Royal Family. His name was Dr Collins. He said Mum was in a coma, which made Grandad gasp and sit right back down. Then the doctor came out with all these medical terms that I didn't understand.

'When will my mum come out of the coma?' I blurted, my head feeling dizzy with all the stuff he was saying.

'She's sustained a severe trauma to the brain so at this moment we can't be sure how long she'll remain unconscious.'

'How can my mum be in a coma?' I said, staring at the doctor as I tried to make sense of this dreadful news.

Malcolm put his arm round me supportively.

'Is she brain-damaged?' asked Grandad, and started crying before Dr Collins could reply.

'I'm afraid it's just too early to say. There are signs that she has some swelling on the brain, which we'll be monitoring over the next twenty-four hours. But apart from that she didn't sustain any other injuries.'

'I can't believe it. I just can't believe it. My poor, poor Rio,' said Grandad, putting his head in his hands.

'Can we see her?' said Auntie Rhona.

The doctor nodded. As we walked to her ward my heart was beating like an elephant stampede. I was desperate to see Mum; but then, there was a part of me that was scared in case she looked like she did this morning, all lifeless. In my head I tried to imagine her sitting up in the bed, smiling cheerfully and telling us off for looking miserable and calling me by my proper name, Isobel, which she only calls me when I've made her cross – like when I haven't put out the bins or tidied up my bedroom or screwed the toothpaste top back on. But I wouldn't mind if she was cross with me if only she'd be healthy and awake.

The nurses had put Mum in a room by herself. She looked helplessly fragile with tubes coming out of her nose and arm. One tube was hooked up to a machine that was beeping and another was connected to a drip. She was no longer in her wedding dress; she'd been changed into a blue hospital gown. Malcolm was the first to rush up to the bed, kissing Mum on the cheek and holding her hand, while Auntie Rhona held her other hand. I wanted to do the same, but it was so scary seeing Mum like that, so I hung back.

'Do you think she can hear us?' I asked Grandad, blinking back the tears that were pricking at my eyes.

'Maybe,' he whispered. 'They do say that people in comas often hear what's being said to them. Why don't you go up and talk to her, Izzy?'

I wasn't sure what to say, which was weird because normally I can talk to my mum about anything, but I guess this wasn't exactly a normal situation.

'Mum, can you hear me? It's Izzy—' I said hesitantly, as I wandered up to the bed.

'Go on, say something else,' Grandad encouraged.

'Um . . . OK. Mum . . . please . . . please get better soon because if you don't then Malcolm will have to do the cooking and, well, we all know that he can't cook,' I tried to joke, even though I didn't feel like laughing.

Malcolm did, but his eyes were all watery with tears.

'Yes, you need to get better soon, my darling, because I don't think Izzy will want pickles on toast every day.' He gently stroked Mum's cheek. 'I'm sure she'd much rather your lovely Thai green curry.'

'Yeah. I want you out of your coma, Mum, ASAP, so you can make me some yummy Thai green curry.'

Grandad spoke to Mum, and so did Auntie Rhona. Grandad told her about Vince arriving drunk, but he didn't seem as angry about it as he did earlier on. Malcolm told Mum that he still couldn't wait to marry her and that as soon as she was well he'd book the church again. Auntie Rhona told Mum that she'd love us to come to San Diego again for another holiday.

'I've never been to California before,' said Malcolm, 'so Rio and I would love to take you up on that offer, wouldn't we, darling?'

He stared at Mum, his eyes literally willing her to reply, but of course she didn't. Before we left, a nurse gave us Mum's wedding dress. It had been folded up and put into a carrier bag. It was a tough moment for all of us. I tried my best not to cry again, but it was all too much for Auntie Rhona, she was in floods of tears. We took a taxi back to the house and were met by music coming from the kitchen. It felt all wrong listening to upbeat music at a moment like this – like a ghost of that morning was taunting us with the happiness we'd felt before Mum's accident. Was it only this morning? I couldn't believe that one day could be so long, or so sad.

We were all exhausted.

'*I'll* sleep down here tonight,' said Malcolm. 'Rhona, you can take mine and Rio's room tonight.'

'Are you sure?' she said to him.

'Yeah, it's all yours,' he responded. 'It's been a difficult day, but let's all try and get some sleep.'

He gave me a hug. 'Please don't worry, Izzy. Your mum will be out of that coma before you know it.'

Then we all hugged each other.

It was hard getting off to sleep. I took my key ring to bed with me and held it tightly as I wished for my mum to be OK. But I was still very shaken up by the day's events and I just couldn't get the image of Mum lying unconscious in the hall out of my head. So I tried to imagine the day as it should have been, a happy day: Mum walking towards the altar looking radiant; her and Malcolm exchanging their rings and wedding vows; the guests at the reception tucking into the sumptuous roast lamb dinner; Mum and Malcolm having their first dance as I sing 'What A Wonderful World'; Mum throwing her bouquet and causing a scrum amongst the single women as they try to catch it; Mum and Malcolm leaving to go on their honeymoon to Portugal. I finally fell asleep.

Five

I could smell breakfast before I'd even stepped out of my bedroom. As I went downstairs, I so wished it was Mum making it and that her accident had simply been a horrible dream. It was Grandad who'd made breakfast: fried eggs, toast and ham. He already had my plate ready at the kitchen table where Auntie Rhona and Malcolm were eating in silence. Grandad and Malcolm gave me a hug.

'Did you sleep all right?' Malcolm asked as I sat down.

'No, not really,' I replied sullenly.

'I didn't, either,' said Auntie Rhona. 'You should've been on your honeymoon now, Malcolm.'

'And we're still going to go on that honeymoon,' said Malcolm, looking at both me and Auntie Rhona. 'Once she's better, we'll get married just as we'd planned.'

'We're all going to go up to the hospital after breakfast,' Grandad told me. 'I called the hospital a short while ago, but there's been no change unfortunately.'

'Well, hopefully she'll be out of that coma today, Grandad,' I said, trying to be positive, but as I took up a forkful of egg and began to eat, it felt like I was swallowing a stone, my stomach still feeling sore from all the worrying.

I tried my best to eat some more, but I couldn't finish it. When we were all washed and changed, Malcolm drove us to the hospital. Grandad spent the journey on his mobile, speaking to relatives and giving them an update on Mum. But each time he'd let them know she was in a coma the phone would go quiet at the other end.

'Hello? Hello?' Grandad found himself saying more than once to check that the person was still there. And when the relative did respond, I could hear the muffled sound of crying. They all said they'd visit Mum at the hospital and a few asked if there was anything they could do to help us out. Belinda offered to do our weekly shop and Kevin said he'd drive us anywhere we wanted to go, even though we have a car. Grandad turned down their offers, but thanked them anyway.

We stopped at a flower stall outside the hospital before going in. 'We should get Mum daisies, she likes daisies,' I said to Auntie Rhona as she scrutinized the assortment of flowers on display.

'Sure, let's get those,' she replied as she took some pink ones out of one of the buckets.

I thought the flowers would brighten up Mum's room, but sadly they didn't do anything for the gloomy beige walls and ugly grey floor. Plus there was no vase to put them in so Auntie Rhona ended up laying the flowers on the windowsill still in the newspaper they'd been wrapped in.

'Will my mum come out of her coma today?' I asked the nurse who was checking Mum's drip.

'It's hard to tell at this stage. Your mum's very ill so right now we're continuing to monitor her closely,' the nurse said. 'But I'm sure she'd be pleased to know that you're all here giving your love and support.'

'Is Dr Collins here today?' enquired Malcolm.

'Yes he is. Would you like to speak to him?'

Malcolm nodded and he and Grandad followed her out the room.

Auntie Rhona pulled up a chair next to Mum's bed and started chatting to her while I hovered behind. She was trying to be upbeat, but her voice croaked with emotion. First she told Mum how she was planning to redecorate her bathroom back in the States, either burnt orange or wisteria. Then she started rambling on about a random health spa for dogs that her assistant Melissa had emailed her about. Even though Mum's eyes were closed, she showed Mum her Blackberry to prove that it was all true.

'Apparently the spa has a Jacuzzi and they do massages and even doggy manicures. I think Tofu would love it,' she laughed lightly then turned round. 'Why don't you come and chat to her, Izzy? I'm sure she'd love to hear your voice.'

'But I wouldn't know what to say.'

'Just say what's on your mind and come in a bit closer so she can hear you.'

So I came out from behind her chair and went up to the bed.

'Maybe I could tell her what we had for breakfast this morning,' I said a bit indecisively.

'Yeah, why not,' said Auntie Rhona.

'Grandad made breakfast this morning, Mum,' I started. 'It was nice but I didn't manage to eat all of it.'

I carefully rested myself on the bed, making sure there was enough space between me and Mum's legs so I wasn't sitting on her.

'He made lots of fried eggs.'

'Too many if you ask me,' Auntie Rhona chipped in with a chuckle.

'What did you have for breakfast, Mum?' I said, but then felt foolish for asking such a question. Then again, why was I even asking her questions when she couldn't respond? I got up.

'I don't feel like talking to her,' I said to Auntie Rhona.

She nodded, but I could tell from the look in her eyes she was thinking of something else for me to do.

'Why don't you sing to her, Izzy?' she said.

'Sing?'

'Yes. I'm sure she'd appreciate it, but only if you want to.'

So that's what I did, sing, but it wasn't easy because after a long think I decided to sing 'What A Wonderful World'. But I tried my hardest not to get upset because I wanted to sing the song as best as I could. I thought, I hoped, that my singing would make her wake up. Before I started I took a few deep breaths just like I told Grandad to do when he was worrying about his wedding speech. I let the air completely fill my lungs before I breathed it all out and then quietly I began the first verse. But as I sang I could feel tears gathering in my throat and my voice began to crack so I stopped.

'You OK?' said Auntie Rhona.

I nodded then took another deep breath. I started again. This time I was determined not to cry and, as I was singing, I was hoping with all my heart that Mum would open her eyes, but sadly she didn't, and I ended the song with a sigh of disappointment.

'That was really good, Izzy. You truly have a gift for singing,' said Auntie Rhona, clapping softly when I was done.

'I thought hearing me would make her wake up,' I muttered.

'She will wake up, sweetie, I'm sure of it,' said Auntie Rhona as Grandad and Malcolm came back in.

'What did the doctor say?' said Auntie Rhona swiftly.

'When does he think Mum will come out of her coma?' I added.

'He said the swelling has started going down, but he couldn't give us an indication of when she's likely to wake up,' said Malcolm, letting out a heavy sigh. 'But we all need to stay optimistic. Rio's a fighter, and when she does wake up she's going to need all of us to be strong for her.'

'I'll try to be strong,' I mumbled, but right then I certainly didn't feel strong. Instead, I felt very, very scared.

Six

I didn't have to go to school on Monday, not that I actually wanted to go 'cos I know I wouldn't have been able to concentrate. Malcolm called my school and told them what had happened and they agreed to let me have three days off so I spent all of Monday, Tuesday and Wednesday at the hospital.

I'd started finding it easier to talk to Mum. I was speaking to her as if we were at the kitchen table drinking tea and eating chocolate digestives. The only difference – she didn't talk back. I told her about all the stuff that had been happening in the soaps and other TV shows she'd missed and I told her about Malcolm's attempt to make a cheese and sardine frittata for dinner one evening, which didn't quite go to plan 'cos the heat was too high and the frittata got burned to a crust. And I let her know that I'd been keeping my room extra tidy, which was something she regularly nags me about, and that I was washing the dishes after dinner, something I rarely ever do, and that I'd put out the bins as well and had remembered to throw all the plastic items into the recycling bin rather than the general waste one, just like she always did. I normally hated doing chores, but I was eager to show Mum that I was being the best daughter I could be.

Grandad decided he'd read to Mum and brought along various newspapers and magazines. But all the stuff he read was so boring. He read her stuff from his golf magazine and he read her chapters from *Sense and Sensibility*, a book by Jane Austen he was currently reading. But it was the Portuguese translation and although I can speak some Portuguese I didn't know enough of the language to get the gist of the story. Auntie Rhona chatted a lot too, mainly about her interior design business and Tofu.

Malcolm was the only one who didn't speak to Mum. His lips moved, but nothing ever came out.

As I can't lip-read I have no idea what he was saying to her. At first I thought his silent talking was kind of dumb until Grandad said it was his way of getting some alone time with Mum. I could understand that 'cos none of us could get any private time with her, not with all the visitors she was getting.

Mum's friends from work popped by with flowers and grapes, so did our next door neighbours Charlotte and Jamie, as well as plenty of our relatives, bearing more armfuls of fruit and flowers. In fact, there were so many flowers and punnets of fruit that we could've turned the room into a florist and a greengrocer's.

When Thursday came I really didn't feel ready to go back to school. I desperately wanted to go back to the hospital and be with Mum, but Malcolm and Grandad thought it was for the best that I went in.

'I think you need a break from the hospital,' said Grandad to me, 'plus going to school will help take your mind off things.'

So on Thursday morning, as always, I put my notepads and books into my bag, slung it over my shoulder and took the bus to school. It felt so strange going off to school without Mum giving me her usual kiss goodbye and asking me if I'd done my homework – I'd always sigh and insist that I had when really I hadn't.

But at school it was good to see Layla, Holly and Alice, who all greeted me with a hug. And as usual Layla gave me half of her Twix. We then went and sat on the bench next to the art block, the place where we usually hang out between classes.

'How are you feeling?' asked Layla.

My friends already knew my mum was in a coma. I'd told Layla on Monday and asked her to let Holly and Alice know as well.

'If my mum wasn't in a coma, I'd be feeling fine,' I replied, as Pippa Barton, a girl in Year Nine walked past, bopping her head to whatever was playing on her iPod. 'These last few days have been awful and none of the doctors seem to know when my mum will wake up. But I'm trying to stay positive.'

'Yeah, you should definitely stay positive,' said Alice considerately.

'Iz,' said Holly, biting her lip. 'Do you think you'll still be able to rehearse the song with us for the party?'

'Holly!' hissed Layla, glowering at her. 'This isn't the time to be talking about my party. It's probably the last thing on Izzy's mind right now.'

'But we've only had one rehearsal. We need to make sure our harmonies are good.'

I wasn't that surprised Holly was worrying about our routine; she was always worrying about something or other. Normally it'd be silly stuff like a spot growing on her chin, or the vegetable lasagne at lunch having too many carrots in it. We'd always tell her to chill out, but this time I thought her worrying was justified, we did need to rehearse a lot more before the party.

'I'm sorry I haven't been around for us to rehearse,' I said quietly.

'You don't have to apologise,' said Layla, putting her arm round my shoulder.

'But I do think we should definitely rehearse as soon as possible 'cos how else are we gonna smash it? Holly's right, we need to make sure our harmonies are up to scratch. Plus it'd be nice to get to do something that's normal and fun after spending all my time at the hospital.'

'Well, why don't we rehearse this Saturday?' said Holly.

Layla shook her head. 'I can't. I have to visit my auntie in Manchester.'

'Then what about next Saturday?' said Holly, her blue eyes wide with anticipation.

'Would you be OK with next Saturday, Iz?' said Layla, her face taut with concern.

'Yeah, next Saturday's fine.'

'We could have the rehearsal at my house,' said Alice, wrapping a strand of her curly black hair round her finger. 'I could get my mum to order us some pizzas so we could have a rehearsal slash pizza party.'

'Cool, I'm up for that,' said Layla, flicking her red hair over her shoulder.

'Yeah, me too,' said Holly.

'And me.' I smiled my first smile in what felt like ages.

It was supposed to have been a private chat with my friends but by lunch time it seemed as though the whole school knew about my mum's accident, all thanks to that nosy parker Pippa Barton. It seems she hadn't been listening to her iPod, but had been busy eavesdropping on our conversation. Loads of kids kept coming up to me, many I didn't know, wanting to know if it was true my mum was in a coma.

Layla, Holly and Alice had to literally act as my bodyguards, warning them off. Layla even found herself having to swear at these boys in Year Seven who asked me if my mum was going to die, which was just horrible. But there were a couple of kids who were much kinder, like Sam Joyner. Today was actually the first time Sam had ever spoken to me even though we're in the same French class. He started telling me about his uncle who'd once been involved in a motorbike accident.

'He was in a coma too, but he recovered completely and he's totally fine now,' he said to me. 'So I'm sure your mum will come out of her coma.'

The only thing I could say to Sam was 'thanks'. I would've liked to have said more, but I was so shy that my mouth just completely dried up. It felt really weird being back at school, not just because of the kids who'd come up to me, but it was like my teachers had all had a personality transplant. They were all being super nice. Even my history teacher, Mrs Boyd, who I swear loves nothing better than to shout at me whenever I miss a deadline for homework, didn't seem to mind that I hadn't even begun my history homework that was four days late.

Layla invited me round to hers for tea. At first I wasn't sure whether to go, thinking it was more important to head straight to the hospital, but when I called Malcolm to tell him he told me I should go to Layla's. He also said there'd been no change in Mum's condition; she was still in a coma.

Layla's mum and her six-year-old brother, Alfie, were in when we got to her house. Alfie's sweet, most of the time, but sometimes he can be a right pain in the neck. He's always getting up to mischief – breaking things and wiping his bogeys everywhere. And he's got a thing for keeping worms as pets and one afternoon, when Layla got home from school, Alfie had put a worm in her bed. Yuck.

'I'm so sorry to hear about your mum,' Layla's mum said to me. 'It was such a shock when your mum's cousin Kevin told us in the church. But since the accident we've been keeping your mum in our thoughts. We hope she wakes up soon.'

Layla's mum let me and Layla have tea in Layla's bedroom. She'd made spaghetti and meatballs which tasted really nice. That's one thing I particularly like about going round Layla's house – her mum always cooks lovely meals. I've been best friends with Layla since primary school when we were put next to each other in Mrs McCurdy's class in reception. I'd love for us to still be friends for as long as Mum and Auntie Rhona have been – maybe Layla and I could even be bridesmaids at each other's weddings.

Although I do consider Holly and Alice to also be my best friends, I'm just that much closer to Layla as I've known her the longest. Back when we were little, we'd sit in Layla's room colouring pictures or combing our Barbies' hair and chat about all the boys we hated, which was literally every boy we knew. We used to regard them as being smelly idiots, but these days our opinion of boys has totally changed. Now Layla's mega obsessed with boys, or should I say, one boy, the actor Chase Dooley. He's the star of these films we like called *The Citrine Chronicles* – he plays the leader of a clever group of kids called the Citrine Legion in a world where every country is at war and desperate to steal the brains of the most intelligent children to put into robot soldiers called BRC2s.

'I tweeted Chase yesterday to ask him if could come to my party,' said Layla, her green eyes shining.

'Did he tweet back?' I asked.

'No, but he will,' she responded confidently.

Layla was always tweeting Chase on Twitter even though he'd never replied. He does, however, have two million followers so it would probably be hard for him to spot Layla's tweets among all the other tweets he must get.

'But isn't Chase filming the fourth film in the Chronicles?' I said. 'Won't he be too busy to come?'

I didn't want to hurt Layla's feelings, but she was totally deluding herself if she really thought that a big movie star like Chase was going to fly all the way from Hollywood to come to our little town for her party in the local community centre. She stood more chance of growing wings and a tail than getting Chase to turn up.

'He is, but you never know, he might come over. And in my tweets I always let him know that I'm his biggest fan. I've also asked him if he could send me a tweet wishing me a happy birthday, which would totally make up for it if he couldn't come.'

'Well, I hope he does come,' I said politely, even though I was certain he wouldn't.

'That was nice of Sam to come up to you today and tell you about his uncle,' said Layla.

'Yeah, it was. I just wish I'd actually said more to him. But I was so nervous, Layla, 'cos he's just so good-looking.'

'He's not as good-looking as Chase, but I s'pose he's kinda cute!' She grinned. 'Why don't you wanna tell Holly and Alice that you fancy Sam? It's not as if they're gonna spread it or anything.'

'I know they wouldn't, but I guess I'm just a little embarrassed 'cos it's not as if Sam is ever going to ask me out. So the fewer people who know the better.'

'I reckon he'll ask you out, but maybe *you* should ask him out.'

'I can't do that!' I balked, my cheeks flushing at the very thought. There's no way I'd have the confidence to do it.

'But I think he really likes you. I mean, did you notice the way he was looking at you today? He was properly staring into your eyes just like how I'd want Chase to stare into mine, all lustful and in love.'

'Don't tease, Layla,' I said, elbowing her playfully. 'He wasn't looking into my eyes.'

'Yes, he was!'

'But not in the way you describe it.'

'Well, I do think he likes you, seriously.'

'Yeah, yeah,' I said, rolling my eyes.

I was glad I went to Layla's house, because for a few hours I didn't have to think about my worries.

Two days later Auntie Rhona had to fly back to the States. She was really gutted she had to go and was crying heaps at the hospital as she said goodbye to Mum, and was crying again at the airport when me and Malcolm waved her off.

'Promise me you'll call as soon as there's been a change in her condition. And please tell Rio I'll be thinking of her every day,' she said before disappearing into the crowd.

I was going to miss Auntie Rhona and I knew Mum would've missed her too.

Seven

My mum woke up a week later on Friday afternoon. I was playing Angry Birds on my phone, and Grandad was reading Mum a newspaper article about a cat called Bluebell who went missing when her owner took her on holiday to the Lake District. Six months later, Bluebell was reunited with her owner after walking an impressive four hundred miles to get back.

'What a clever cat managing to find its home from such a long way away,' Grandad was saying.

'Cat?' Mum muttered. Grandad dropped his newspaper. I almost dropped my iPhone.

'Mum, you're awake!' I said, rushing up to the bed.

Her eyes were only a little bit open but she was awake all right.

'Dad,' she gurgled.

'Yes, I'm here, sweetheart,' said Grandad, smiling hugely. 'I was so frightened that you'd never wake up, but it's so good to have you back with us.'

'I've missed you so much,' I said to her, feeling overwhelmed with both happiness and relief.

My mum was finally out of her coma; she was going to be OK. Me and Grandad hugged each other joyfully.

'Where . . . where am I?' Mum croaked, her eyelids flickering.

'You're in the hospital, Rio,' said Grandad, taking hold of her hand. 'You had an accident. You hit your head.'

'There's something in my nose,' she whispered.

'Yes, it's a tube, sweetheart. You've been in a coma but I'm going to go and get the doctor now and let him know that you're awake.'

He left the room.

'Oh, Mum, I'm so happy you're awake,' I sobbed and held her hand. 'When you get home, you won't have to lift a finger because me, Malcolm and Grandad, we're all going to look after you. I'll do all the cleaning round the house and ironing and I'll always keep my bedroom tidy, which I've already started doing; you don't have to worry about it being messy any more. I'll mow the lawn, even if the grass pollen gives me the sneezes, I'll do whatever is needed so you can concentrate on getting better.' But I don't think she was listening. I didn't mind, though, she was awake and that's all I cared about right then.

She was very drowsy, her eyes closing and reopening. Grandad came back in the room with Dr Collins and a nurse.

'Izzy, let's pop outside while the doctor checks your mum over,' said Grandad.

'OK,' I said reluctantly. I joined him in the corridor, even though I didn't want to leave Mum's side for a moment. I gave Grandad a big smile and another hug. I was so relieved.

'When do you think she'll be able to come home, Grandad, now that she's awake?' I asked him.

'Well, I imagine the doctors will want her to stay here for a little while longer, but as soon as she's ready we'll take her home.'

'I should let Malcolm know she's awake,' I said suddenly. 'He's going to be so happy, Grandad.'

I quickly began writing out a text on my phone.

Good news – Mum's woken up :)

Malcolm was still at work, but hopefully once he'd seen the text he'd come straight to the hospital.

After about fifteen minutes Dr Collins came back out with the nurse.

'Can we see her?' I asked immediately.

'Course. She's still a bit sleepy, but I'm sure she'd love to see you both,' said Dr Collins as me and Grandad rushed back inside.

'Dad,' Mum murmured to him, her eyes blinking up at him as he approached the bed.

'Yes, I'm here, Rio,' he replied and squeezed her hand.

'You look different,' she said slowly, her eyes resting on his face.

'I expect I do,' said Grandad in Portuguese. 'I haven't had a shave in quite a while. I probably look very scruffy,' he added in English.

'He's been here every day,' I told her, 'and Malcolm's been coming too, but he went back to work today. I usually come after school.'

'Do I... Do I know you?' said Mum, looking towards me.

'Course you do,' I smiled, but wondered why she'd asked such a question.

She looked back at Grandad.

'Old,' she whispered. 'You look old, Dad.'

'Well, I'm definitely not a young man any more, that's for sure,' he grinned. 'Although when I finally have a shave I might look a bit better.'

'What day is it?' asked Mum weakly.

'It's Friday,' I told her.

'School,' she whispered.

'Yes, I went to school today. I didn't get all of my homework in on time 'cos I've been coming here a lot, but I will do it,' I said. 'But I have been doing lots of chores at home; you can ask Grandad if you don't believe me.'

'Yes, she's been helping me take care of the house,' said Grandad, patting me on the shoulder.

'He's your grandad?' said Mum, looking at me again strangely.

'Yes. He's your dad and I'm your daughter.'

'Daughter? I don't have a daughter,' she murmured.

I flinched. 'Y-yes you do. Me,' I stuttered.

I looked at Grandad anxiously, my heart thumping in my chest.

Why would Mum say such a thing?

'Rio, you do know this is Izzy?' said Grandad slowly.

I gulped as I waited for her to answer.

'I don't know any Izzy and I've never seen this girl before in my life.'

It was as if someone had slapped me across the face. I felt totally shocked and stung by her words.

How could my own mum say that?

'She is your daughter, Rio, and you are her mum,' said Grandad, his voice shaking and his face looking as shocked as I felt.

Mum looked at him oddly.

'How can I be her mum when I'm only fourteen?' she mumbled.

'You *are* my mum,' I said to her, but then I realised what she'd just said: fourteen! Had she lost her memory?

I pulled Grandad to one side.

'She doesn't remember me, Grandad,' I muttered, feeling close to tears. 'I think she has . . .'

'Amnesia,' Grandad answered, taking the words straight out of my mouth, and we both gasped. He took off his glasses and tapped them against the palm of his hand in thought.

'You stay here, Izzy, I'll go and get Dr Collins again.'

He went up to Mum. 'Rio, I'm just going to get Dr Collins,' he told her softly.

'Please don't leave me,' said Mum, her face looking frightened. She grabbed hold of his arm.

'I won't be long, sweetheart, I promise,' he said, gently shaking off her grip before leaving the room, and leaving Mum and me staring at each other in complete astonishment.

I could tell she was trying her hardest to figure out who I was, while I hadn't a clue what to say. I was too shocked to speak. Maybe she was playing a practical joke on me, I thought. Mum was very good at playing pranks – one time she managed to convince a guy at her work that the plant on his desk was magical, when really she'd been replacing the plant with a bigger version whenever he'd popped to the toilet or gone to make himself a coffee. But this time her eyes looked deadly serious, petrified even.

'I am fourteen,' she insisted into the silence, 'and I'm not your mum.'

'I think you've lost your memory, Mum. But Grandad will be back with the doctor in a minute. He'll be able to tell us what's wrong with you,' I said to her, my voice trembling.

'My memory's fine. I am fourteen. I am,' she croaked.

I sat down on one of the easy chairs, my stomach feeling sick with fear as I looked towards the door and silently willed Grandad and Dr Collins to walk in immediately. I needed the doctor to tell me what was wrong with my mum. I needed to make sense of what was happening and I needed him to make her better so she could remember me again.

'I don't see how I can be your mum when you look about twelve,' said Mum.

'I am twelve,' I muttered.

'And I'm fourteen. You can ask my best friend Rhona, she'll tell you.'

'She went back to America. She was here but—'

'America? What's she doing there?'

'She lives over there.'

'No, she doesn't,' said Mum. 'She lives on Cavendish Road, number twenty-six.'

'She lives in America with Tofu, her dog,' I said, my voice catching in my throat; the joy I was feeling only a short while ago now turned into panic.

'No, she lives here in Top Hill,' said Mum, shaking her head disbelievingly.

I got up and walked over to her.

'She came over to see you marry Malcolm, only you never got married 'cos of your accident. You fell down the stairs. Do you remember that? Can you remember anything?'

'No, I don't remember having an accident and I don't know any Malcolm either, and why would I get married when I'm only fourteen?'

Grandad walked in with Dr Collins.

'Hi, sweetheart, the doctor's here. He just wants to have a little chat and check you over,' he whispered.

'She thinks she's fourteen,' I blurted. 'She's definitely lost her memory.'

'Is that correct, Rio?' said Dr Collins to Mum. 'You think you're fourteen?'

'Yes, I am fourteen,' said Mum and was now looking as confused and as scared as I was feeling.

'Tell me, what's the last thing you remember?' asked Dr Collins.

'I went to school, I came home. Dad got us fish and chips for dinner. He had it all wrapped up when he came home from work. We watched some telly and then I went to bed.'

'And can you tell me if you recognise Izzy?' said Dr Collins, pointing towards me.

'No, I don't know who she is and I don't want her here, either. I want her to go!'

I burst into tears.

'Come on, Izzy, let's go and get some fresh air,' said Grandad. 'I'll be back soon, Rio,' he told Mum, and then we both left the room.

We went right out of the hospital building and sat on a bench near the entrance.

'I can't believe she doesn't remember me, Grandad,' I cried. 'What are we going to do?'

'Well, the first thing we need to do is not panic and wait to see what the doctor says,' he replied, putting his arm round me. 'Maybe it's something that will pass in a few hours, these things are often temporary.'

Just then I spotted Malcolm getting out of his car. He waved at us and began to walk over.

'What are you both doing out here?' he said as he approached us, a bright smile on his face. 'I thought you'd be with Rio now that she's woken up. I can't wait to see her.'

'We've got something to tell you, Malcolm,' I said. I looked at Grandad hesitantly.

'What is it? Have you been crying, Izzy?' he said, a look of worry suddenly spreading across his face. 'Oh no, has something happened? Please tell me she's all right, your text said—'

'It seems Rio has some kind of amnesia,' Grandad cut in. 'She couldn't remember Izzy and she thinks she's fourteen.'

'She didn't remember Izzy...gosh,' said Malcolm, covering his mouth in astonishment.

'The doctor's with her at the moment,' said Grandad.

'But has the doctor actually confirmed that it's amnesia?' asked Malcolm.

'No but...'

'Well let's not panic yet, Julius,' said Malcolm. 'Right now I'm just glad she's out of the coma.'

Malcolm led the way back in, walking hurriedly to Mum's room. Dr Collins was with Mum when we returned. He was with a nurse called Jenny who had curly red hair and a small tattoo of a mermaid on her arm. I liked Jenny and thought she was the nicest of all the nurses who'd been taking care of Mum.

'The doctor thinks I have amnesia,' said Mum to Grandad.

'Yes, sweetheart, I think you do,' he said gently.

'But my memory's fine. I'm fourteen, Dad, I am,' Mum persisted, then turned her attention to Malcolm, eyeing him warily. 'Who are you?'

Malcolm looked completely crushed. 'It's me, Rio,' he muttered, but it was obvious from the look on her face that she hadn't a clue who he was.

Dr Collins pulled Grandad and Malcolm aside. He told them he thought Mum was suffering from something called post-traumatic amnesia and that they'd be giving her a brain scan to confirm this.

'How long does amnesia last?' I asked Nurse Jenny.

'It's hard to tell, I'm afraid,' she replied in a low voice. 'It could be a couple of days to a couple of weeks; although sometimes it can be a lot longer.'

I gasped. Was my mum going to be stuck like this for ever?

'But hopefully your mum's memory loss is just temporary,' she added.

'Why does my mum think she's fourteen? Is that what happens to people with amnesia, they think they're a different age?' I asked her.

'Amnesia is a complex condition and Dr Collins has said that, yes, in some cases it can cause some people to believe that they're a different age from what they really are.'

'And how will my mum's memories come back? Will she need to have an operation or something?'

'Well, normally a person's memories come back all by themselves, but there will be support offered to your mum to help her relearn things she's forgotten. You'll just have to be very patient and supportive.' She gave me a reassuring smile.

'Dad, the doctor said the year is 2014,' Mum croaked from the bed.

'Yes, Rio, it *is* 2014,' said Grandad drifting back towards her.

'So it isn't 1995?' A solitary tear crept down Mum's face. She wiped it away with her hand and began touching the whole of her face. 'My face . . . it feels different.'

'It would do,' said Grandad.

'Do you have a mirror, Jenny?' asked Dr Collins.

'Yes I do, Doctor,' she replied, pulling out a compact mirror from her pocket.

‘I think Rio needs to see herself,’ said Dr Collins to Grandad, taking the mirror from Jenny and giving it to him.

Grandad nodded and slowly opened the mirror in front of Mum.

‘This is you, Rio,’ he said in Portuguese. ‘You’re not fourteen any more, sweetheart.’

For a moment there was complete silence as Mum gazed at her reflection, her deep brown eyes, the freckles across her nose. And then the silence was shattered by a wail of anguish.

‘That can’t be me! That can’t be!’ she muttered.

‘It *is* you, sweetheart,’ said Grandad, crying. ‘You’re a grown woman, Rio.’

‘But I look so old,’ Mum wept.

‘Nonsense, you’re not old,’ he replied, pretending to giggle, but tears were raining down his face. ‘You’re a woman in your prime, that’s what you are.’

‘But I don’t want to be a woman,’ sobbed Mum. ‘I want to be fourteen!’ She suddenly tried to get up. ‘This is not really happening; it’s all a dream.’

‘Rio, please don’t get up. It’s important you don’t exert yourself,’ said Dr Collins.

'Yes, Mum, you have to rest,' I told her, but she took no notice.

'I need to wake up from this dream,' she continued and pinched her arm. 'I'm not waking up!'

'You are awake, darling,' said Malcolm.

'Don't call me darling. I don't even know who you are,' she snapped at him.

'I'm your fiancé.'

'No, you're not. I don't have a fiancé and as if I'd marry you,' said Mum. 'You've got lanky legs and cross-eyes.'

Malcolm was tall, but he definitely didn't have cross-eyes. But it was obvious Mum had upset him with her cruel remark; his shoulders drooped.

'And what's that silly T-shirt you're wearing?' said Mum, trying to read the slogan that was on it. '"This is not a bag, this is a T-shirt". Well of course it's a T-shirt. Blooming hell, I don't need to be told that it's one.'

'You love my T-shirts,' muttered Malcolm bleakly.

'I just don't get it,' said Mum. 'How could I have aged in the space of a few hours? Last night I went to my bed, in my bedroom with my posters from *Girl Zone* magazine all around me. And today I'm in hospital and this doctor's telling me I'm thirty-three.'

'As I said, Rio, a severe trauma to the brain can often lead to memory loss, it's not uncommon,' said Dr Collins.

'Is there any medication she can take to bring back her memories?' asked Grandad.

'I'm afraid not, Mr Silva. But we can see about getting Rio some therapy to help her come to terms with all of this.'

'And we'll help her too,' I said to Dr Collins. 'We'll help you remember all the things you've forgotten,' I said, looking at Mum. 'Like me,' I added under my breath.

'I told you, I don't want that girl in here,' said Mum. 'I don't want her anywhere near me. Get him out too,' she said as she glared at Malcolm.

'But they're your family, Rio, who you love very much,' said Grandad.

'But how can I love them when I don't know who they are?'

I'd never seen my mum look at me with such disdain. It made my stomach twist with hurt.

'Do you remember the day I proposed to you?' said Malcolm to Mum suddenly. 'We had a picnic in the park and sat under a tree that you said looked like a man standing on one leg. And there was a dog, a little Yorkie that came and stole a few of our cocktail sausages. And the ring . . . you found it at the bottom of the picnic basket where I'd hidden it. You said yes immediately. Please tell me you remember.' He looked at Mum desperately.

'I don't remember that,' said Mum. 'I don't know you.'

'Well what about that evening when we went to a fan screening night of *Star Wars*? We both dressed up. I went as Han Solo and you were Princess Leia.'

'What? I don't know what you're talking about. Please just go,' Mum shrieked.

Malcolm let out a heavy sigh. He turned and walked out.

'I want you to go as well,' Mum growled at me.

'But I want to stay here with you. Please, Mum,' I said, my eyes going misty with tears.

'I'm not your mum and I never want to be your mum,' she said cuttingly.

'I'm sure she doesn't mean that,' said Nurse Jenny, looking at me sympathetically.

'I do mean it,' said Mum.

'Rio, you can't say that. She is your child! Surely

you can see the resemblance – the nose, the eyes. She looks exactly like you,' said Grandad.

Mum looked at me again, her face searching mine and I desperately hoped she could see the resemblance.

'She, um, does a bit . . .' she started.

'Does what, Rio?' asked Grandad.

'Looks like me, well, how I thought I looked, anyway,' she replied quietly.

'Yes, that's because she's your daughter,' said Grandad.

'No, she's not and I don't want her to be, I want nothing to do with her!'

'She's only saying those things, Izzy, because she's not well. You have to understand that,' said Grandad, trying to comfort me.

But I didn't understand and ran out the room.

'She thinks it's 1995,' Malcolm rasped. He was sitting in the corridor, his eyes wide with bewilderment. 'And any feelings she once had for me – they've vanished, just like that.'

'She doesn't love *me* any more, Malcolm,' I sniffed.

'Hey, come on, you know that's not true. She loves you more than anything in the world,' he said, standing up and giving me a hug. 'Look, she might not know who we are, but your mum's going to need us more than ever now, Izzy. We have to help her get through this.'

Eight

I didn't feel like doing the dance rehearsal the next day, but I also didn't want to let my friends down. They were ever so excited about it and couldn't wait to get started as soon as I got to Alice's. I was the last to turn up after spending most of the day moping about the house. I'd wanted to go back to the hospital to see if I could get Mum to remember me, but Grandad thought it was best that me and Malcolm 'gave her some space' to avoid her getting all worked up again, so he went to the hospital by himself. Before he left, he got a phone call from the hospital to confirm that Mum did have amnesia and my heart sank.

I was feeling pretty blue and I'm sure Malcolm was too, but he was doing his best to stay upbeat and, before I left to go to Alice's, he made me this grilled sandwich called Croque Monsieur to cheer me up. It did taste much nicer than the experimental type of sandwiches he normally likes to make, but unfortunately it didn't do the trick, I still felt miserable.

As I walked to Alice's I wondered whether to tell my friends about Mum's amnesia. When I arrived at her house, though, I decided not to because I knew I'd just burst into tears, completely ruining the happy mood everyone was in. So when my friends asked me how she was, I simply told them she was out of her coma and was 'much better' and they were all really pleased for me. Layla wanted us to start rehearsing straightaway. She was super excited and had even come dressed as Jesy from Little Mix, wearing a pair of Aztec-patterned trousers, a denim waistcoat and big hoop earrings, whereas the rest of us were just in T-shirts and leggings. She also took charge of the choreography.

'Alice, when I step forward, you need to step back, then we all clap our hands,' said Layla, 'and the bit where we sing "fly", we need to all jump back then march forward like soldiers. No, not like that, Alice, you have to move your hands like you're beating a drum.'

But it was Holly who was getting confused with the steps and kept forgetting the lyrics, which frustrated Layla.

'We're not getting this right, girls,' she said to us, exasperated after only thirty minutes. Holly, who'd been the one looking forward to the rehearsal the most, now didn't look so happy. In fact she looked completely fed up.

'I'm trying my best, Layla,' she moaned. 'And you're not explaining the steps properly; you're just bossing us about.'

'Am not! Look, I just want us to be perfect otherwise we're just gonna look like idiots,' said Layla.

'Are you calling us idiots?' said Alice, her face furious.

It was the first time I'd ever seen Alice look cross. She's the quietest out of the four of us and normally the one who has the biggest and brightest smile on her face; so to see her so angry was quite a shock. But it was clear that she and Holly had had enough of Layla's pushy attitude.

Normally Layla's a lot of fun and way more relaxed than she was being today, but ever since her parents agreed to throw her a Sweet Thirteenth birthday party, the whole thing had gone to her head. She was determined to make her party one people would never forget. Her parents were just as determined to go all out and give her exactly what she wanted, which included: a candy floss machine; a massive chocolate fountain; a photo booth that took stylish photos instead of drabby ones; and a limo to take us all there. Her parents had also booked Master Slick, a DJ from London to do the music. Layla said he'd played at all the top nightclubs around the world. So I reckoned it must have cost her parents a fortune to book him. It seemed very over the top to me, but I was looking forward to it, I think we all were. And even though Layla always has whatever she wants, she's really kind and generous and, normally, not at all spoiled about it all.

'Hey, let's not turn this into an argument,' I said quickly. 'All we need to do is keep practising and we'll soon nail the routine.'

My friends shook their heads wearily and we continued to practise. Even though I hadn't been in the mood for dancing or singing, it did help to take my mind off Mum and when we finished our rehearsal, a whole three hours later, it was nice to chat about stuff that wasn't to do with the hospital and my mum's accident.

'I'd love to be in a real girl group like Little Mix,' said Alice, eating a slice of ham and pineapple pizza. 'It would be such a cool job 'cos I'd get to travel the world and perform in front of thousands of people.'

'That's exactly why I want to become a pop star,' I said. 'I want lots of people to come to my concerts and have the time of their lives.'

'And if you do become famous, d'you reckon you'll marry another celebrity 'cos that's what lots of famous people end up doing?' said Alice.

'My sister Violet's always going on about how she wants to get married to someone famous so she can be in all the celebrity magazines, but she'd be so lucky,' said Holly.

'Actually, I think I'd prefer to marry someone that wasn't famous. That way I won't have to have the paparazzi hanging outside my house,' I said.

'You should marry Sam, then. I heard he wants to be a vet when he's older,' said Layla, then quickly covered her mouth.

'Sam? Why did you mention Sam?' Holly asked suspiciously.

I quickly shook my head at Layla.

'Oops,' she muttered.

'Don't tell me you have a crush on Sam,' said Alice, her brown eyes widening.

I bit my lip.

'You do!' she grinned.

'Why are we only finding out about this now?' said Holly, sounding reproachful. 'And how come Layla knew, but me and Alice didn't?'

'I dunno. I suppose I was just kind of embarrassed,' I mumbled, feeling guilty.

I should've known Holly would be the one to be most upset out of my friends. She hates being the last to find out about something.

'But we're your friends, Izzy, or don't you think we're good enough to be told such information?' said Holly, giving me the third degree.

'Course not. I'm sorry, OK?'

'Oh, it's all right, don't stress,' said Alice. 'Although I can see why you fancy him; he's well fit.'

'I know, tell me about it,' I drooled.

'If you and Sam go out, you'll be the first out of

all of us to have a boyfriend,' said Alice. 'Gosh, you're so lucky, Izzy. I wish I had a boyfriend. You have to tell us what it's like kissing him so I can know if kissing is as lovely as they say.'

I blushed. 'Steady on, Alice. Sam doesn't even know I like him yet.' Then I looked at all of them very seriously. 'Promise me that you won't tell him 'cos I think I'd die of embarrassment if he ever found out.'

'Well, if that's what you want then I won't tell,' said Holly.

'Not a word,' said Layla, pretending to zip up her mouth.

'And I won't say anything, either. But seriously, Iz, you shouldn't be scared that you can't tell us something 'cos we're all best friends; we'll always be there for each other no matter what,' said Alice.

When I got back home Malcolm wasn't in but Grandad had returned from the hospital and was making himself a cup of tea in the kitchen.

'How's Mum?' I asked him automatically.

'Fancy a cuppa?'

I shrugged with disinterest, but he started making me one anyway.

'So how is she, Grandad?'

'How did your rehearsal go?' he asked.

'It was OK, I s'pose. Did Mum ask after me?'

Grandad hesitated for a moment then let out a long sigh. 'No, sweetheart, she didn't. I'm sorry. She still doesn't know who Malcolm or you are, but she did get introduced to a woman called Karen today. She's a therapist who's worked with lots of people who have suffered amnesia. She's going to start seeing Rio every Tuesday and Wednesday to teach her some skills to help her remember things she's forgotten and support her through this difficult time. Karen said we can also help by showing your mum a diary so she can read about the things she did, places she's been to, that sort of thing.'

'But Mum doesn't keep a diary.'

'In that case, Karen did suggest we could put a scrapbook together and fill it with old photos and other bits and pieces.'

'I could do the scrapbook. There's loads of stuff I could put in it too. So do you think it'll help her get back her memories, Grandad?'

'It might and it might not,' he said in Portuguese. 'But Karen thinks it's something worth doing and she is the expert.'

He handed me my cup of tea.

'I know Mum doesn't want to see me but I really want to see her. I miss her so much, Grandad.'

'I know you do, Izzy. Listen, I'm not expecting her to be very welcoming, but why don't you come up to the hospital tomorrow? I'm really keen for Rio to get to know you again.'

It was such a weird thought that my mum would have to get to know me, but I was willing to try anything to get my mum back. I knew it wasn't going to be easy.

Nine

The following day me, Grandad and Malcolm went to the hospital. Malcolm was dressed as if he were going to a job interview, wearing a smart suit and tie. Grandad told him he just needed to 'be himself', but Malcolm said that he didn't want Mum to think she was going out with a dork. I was dressed casually but I was nervous too. I was worried Mum would tell me to go away like she did when she came out of her coma, and when we reached the hospital I started to fret.

'Maybe I should just stay in the car. She's not going to want to see me, is she, Grandad?'

'I'll have a word with her. Like I said yesterday, it's important that she gets to know you.'

'It's gonna be fine, Izzy. When we go in, why don't you tell your mum about your school and the things you like to do, y'know, how you like to sing? And you could tell her about the stuff that the two of you do together,' said Malcolm.

When we got to Mum's room, Grandad went inside first while Malcolm and I sat outside shuffling our feet awkwardly, like two naughty kids waiting to see the headmistress. After about ten minutes Grandad came back out.

'She wants to see you.'

Malcolm stood up quickly but Grandad shook his head.

'I'm sorry, Malcolm, it's only Izzy she wants to see.'

'Why not me?' he muttered. 'It's been unbearable not being able to see her.'

'The thing is, Malcolm, she's going to need a lot of time to get her head around the fact that she's in a grown-up relationship and isn't a teenage girl, if you understand what I mean,' said Grandad.

'I understand,' said Malcolm, but sighed deeply.

'I'll stay out here with Malcolm, Izzy, so you and your mum can chat,' said Grandad.

So I went into the room alone, loitering by the door, waiting for Mum to summon me forward.

She was sitting up. 'Hello,' she said, but not in a friendly way.

Although she still had a tube coming out of her arm, she looked healthier than she did two days ago.

'Hi,' I said back.

'You can come closer, but if you think I'm going to be your mum then you're living in a dream world. Because I don't want to be *anyone's* mum.' She glared at me as if I were a piece of chewing gum someone had spat on the ground.

'OK,' I said lightly, pretending not to be bothered, but deep down I was.

'Good. I'm glad we've got that sorted,' she said. 'My dad says that I live with you and that Malcolm guy. But he said that he wasn't your dad, another man called Gavin is and he's not around any more.'

'He left us when I was a baby. He went off with someone else,' I told her.

'He doesn't sound very nice,' said Mum. Then her face suddenly turned sad. 'My mum's not around, either. She died when I was ten. I so wish she was here. I wish I could see her again.'

'You always used to tell me how much you loved

her and how much she meant to you. That's why you called me Isobel.'

For a moment Mum didn't say anything. Then she changed the subject. 'Have you seen my hair? I hate it.'

'Well, I think it's lovely, and it's how you wanted Kye to do it.'

'Kye? Who's Kye?'

'Your hairdresser.'

'I have my own hairdresser, do I? Wow, I've never had my own hairdresser before. Did he do your hair as well?'

'Yes.'

'It looks . . . nice.'

'Thanks,' I said, smiling.

My mobile vibrated in my bag. I quickly took it out and checked it. I had a text from Layla.

Thought Chase just followed me on
Twitter. Wasn't Chase just dumb boy
with similar username. So angry.

'What's that?' said Mum.

'It's my mobile,' I replied.

'A mobile phone? Is that what they look like now?'

I nodded.

'I didn't know kids were allowed to have mobile phones.'

'Some aren't but nearly every kid at my school has one. There's a boy in my year called Zoom who has five.'

'Zoom. What kind of daft name is that?'

'Yeah, it is a bit wacky, isn't it? There's also a girl in my year who's called Mystical. And there's a girl in Year Ten whose name is Princess Zemelda but she's not a real princess, her mum just wanted her to be called that.'

'Weird. I feel sorry for them having names like that. Could I erm . . . see your phone?'

I gave it to her.

'That's a strange phone, it doesn't have any buttons,' she said, looking at it curiously.

'That's because it's a touch-screen phone,' I said, leaning over and clicking on my calendar app. 'It's got lots of great apps on it.'

'Apps?' said Mum, looking at me perplexed.

'Yeah, I've got my games, YouTube app, photo apps. I have tons of photos of you on here.'

I quickly slid through my photo album, showing her various photos of herself – relaxing at home, showing off a new handbag, opening a present at Christmas, kissing Malcolm at their engagement party. She was truly stunned.

'That's me,' she gawped like it was the first time she was seeing herself. 'I look so . . . grown up.'

'That's just a couple of photos. I've got loads more. Do you want to see them?'

'No, it's all right,' she breathed. 'Do I have a mobile?'

'Yes, a Blackberry.'

'Blackberry?'

'Yeah, that's the name of it. It's a bit different from my phone. It does have buttons. It's at home but I can bring it in for you tomorrow if you want.'

She shrugged.

'I hardly know anyone with a mobile except for Belinda. But she says you have to be eighteen to get a mobile. She's nineteen. Do you know Belinda? Her mum is Auntie Caroline who's my mum's sister.'

'Yes, I know Belinda, but she's not nineteen any more.'

'Of course, how could I forget,' said Mum, slapping her forehead and pretending to laugh. 'The thing is I really have forgotten that and half my life.'

I didn't know whether to laugh along with her or not. Her laugh sounded a little desperate and sad. I wanted to reach over and comfort her, but I was scared she'd bite my head off if I did.

'And how is Auntie Caroline? I imagine she's really old now.'

'She's good. She and Uncle Bruce live in Spain.'

'Do they?'

'Yeah, they moved there two years ago, but Kevin and Belinda still live here.'

'And tell me, what else has happened in the world? What modern inventions have there been?'

'Well there's the Internet, that was a big invention.'

'I already know about that and it's so slow. They used to have the Internet on one of the computers in the library at my school, but the teachers said we were all mucking about on it so they got rid of it. Rhona and I would go on the Internet sometimes at lunch time and look for photos of actors and pop stars but it used to take for ever to load just one photo.'

'The Internet's much faster now and you can get it on your mobile and you can listen to music and watch films and TV shows on it.'

‘So erm, what school do you go to?’ said Mum, changing the subject again.

‘The same school you went to, Broomwood High.’

She snorted. ‘Eurgh. Why would you want to go there? It’s an awful school. I can’t stand the place.’

‘Really?’ I said, surprised. Mum had always made out she enjoyed her time at Broomwood and that’s why she sent me there. ‘I always I thought you liked Broomwood.’

‘Like it? Nah, you must be thinking of someone else. I hate school, that’s why I spend most of my time bunking off.’

I blinked; my mouth opened wide with astonishment. ‘You skipped school!’

‘Yeah, and?’

‘Friday afternoons are the best time to bunk off,’ said Mum. ‘Me and Rhona go to the park and sometimes to the cinema if we have enough money. So, what else have I missed? Have scientists come up with a machine that cooks food faster than a microwave?’

‘I wouldn’t know, but we do have a microwave at home,’ I responded, still stumped that she used to skip school.

'And what about knee-high boots? Are they still in fashion?'

'Yes. We both have a pair of knee-highs.'

'And is tie-dye still in?'

'I think so.'

All of a sudden she started firing more questions at me which made me feel like a contestant on a quiz show.

'How many TV channels do we have?'

I quickly tried to count the number of channels we had in my head.

'More than four?' said Mum, hurrying me.

'Yes.'

'So do we have cable TV?'

'No, we have Sky.'

'Is *Home & Away* still running?'

'Yes.'

'Has there been a sequel to *E.T.*?'

'No.'

'Is John Major still the prime minster?'

'Who? No, someone else is the prime minster.'

'What's their name?'

'Er...' I did know the name but I just couldn't remember it. Trying to answer her questions at speed made me feel like I'd lost my memory myself.

'Has England won the World Cup again?'

'No.'

'Can cars fly?'

'No.'

'Does McDonald's still make Chicken McNuggets?'

'Yes.'

'Do shops still sell Quavers crisps?'

'Yes.'

'And Pot Noodles?'

'Yes.'

'And Cherry Coke?'

'Um . . . er . . . yes!'

I felt like saying yes, yes, yes to everything just so we could talk about something else. But after that Mum didn't ask any more random questions. I thought she might've asked some questions to find out more about me, but it was clear she was more interested in knowing if cheesy Quavers still existed than trying to get to know me properly.

'My dad says I work as a press officer, not that I know what that is.'

'Yes, you work for the council. You write information about things the council is doing which are called press releases.'

'The job sounds enormously dull,' said Mum, yawning.

'Actually, you really enjoy it. And you've always told me that you prefer it to the clerk job you had at the bank.'

'I worked in a bank as well? Gross. My life sounds like it's turned out to be a right disaster,' said Mum, puffing out her cheeks.

'No, Mum; your life hasn't been a disaster. You're very happy.'

'Look, I know I'm supposed to be your mum, not that I want be, but I'd prefer it if you called me Rio,' she replied stiffly.

I didn't like the idea of calling Mum by her name 'cos it would feel like she wasn't my mum at all, just someone I knew. It also felt rude to call her Rio, but if that's what she wanted, I guessed I was just going to have to do it. I couldn't believe how different my mum was aged fourteen – it was like her amnesia had given her a complete personality transplant.

'So what else can you tell me? Can I drive?'

I shook my head. 'No, you failed your driving test four times.'

Mum frowned. 'Well, do I live in a big house?'

'I suppose it's fairly big. The kitchen's big and we

have three bedrooms that are big-ish.'

'And do I have a swimming pool?'

'I wish! Auntie . . . Rhona has a swimming pool. But in our garden we have a vegetable patch.'

'A vegetable patch, that does sound fun,' Mum mocked. 'What I was hoping you'd say is that I live in a fabulous mansion and that I'm super rich. Rhona sounds like she is. I also hoped I'd be married to Kenny Kennedy, but I guess that hasn't happened, either.'

'Why would you want to be married to Kenny Kennedy?'

'Duh, 'cos I fancy the pants off him, that's why.'

I was confused. It was Auntie Rhona who was supposed to have had the crush on Kenny Kennedy, not Mum.

'But I thought Rhona was the Kenny Kennedy fan.'

'She does like him but not as much as I do. I'm the proper fan. I have all his albums as well as a Kenny Kennedy lunchbox, sweatshirt and baseball cap. Plus I have loads of posters of him in my room.'

'Actually, you don't have any posters of him in your room.'

'Well, I . . . used to. Plus I've met him in real life.

Me and Rhona snuck into his dressing room at one of his concerts.'

'Yeah, I know all about that. He signed a towel for Rhona.'

'He signed it for *me*, you mean. It was my towel, not Rhona's.'

'Really? You always made out that the towel was hers,' I muttered, feeling a bit swamped with all this new stuff I was discovering about my mum.

'So is Kenny still making music?' asked Mum.

I shook my head.

'That's a shame,' she replied wistfully.

Grandad came into the room.

'Hello, Rio. I just popped in to see how your chat's going with Izzy. I'm sure she's been busy filling you in on lots of things.'

'She told me that cars can't fly. I thought the future would be much better than this,' said Mum emphatically.

'Well, it sounds like you had an interesting chat,' said Grandad.

'Yeah, I guess we did.' I smiled at Mum, only she didn't smile back.

'By the way, Rio, Malcolm is still keen to see you,' said Grandad delicately.

'I don't want to see him,' snapped Mum. 'I've told you, I don't know who he is.'

'That's why I think it would be good for you to get to know him, sweetheart,' said Grandad, a tense look spreading across his face as though he was worried he'd said something to upset Mum.

'I don't want to get to know him,' said Mum crisply. 'And when I get home, I want him gone.'

'But our house is his house,' I said. 'You can't chuck him out. Where would he live?'

'I don't care – but he's not living in my home, that's for sure,' said Mum bluntly.

I swallowed and looked at Grandad. 'We can't just chuck Malcolm out.'

'Actually I think it's probably best that he does move out at least temporarily,' said Grandad.

I couldn't believe what Grandad was saying. And it felt so weird hearing Mum being mean about Malcolm, but I realised she must be really frightened and confused. I couldn't imagine waking up one day and finding out I was actually an adult and had a family of my own. I realised it would be hopeless trying to convince Mum to let Malcolm stay. He was now no more than a stranger to her... just like I was.

Ten

Malcolm was heartbroken that Mum wanted him to leave.

'We were about to get married,' he kept saying over and over as he packed a suitcase.

A few days had passed since Grandad had told him the news and I know it had been difficult for Malcolm to take in.

It had been difficult for me too. Malcolm was going to stay with his friend Vince and I didn't want him to go. He might not have been my real dad, but he was the closest that I had to a dad and I loved him dearly.

'I just wish Mum would let you stay,' I kept saying to him.

'I do as well, but don't you get upset about it, Izzy. I'm sure when her memories return she'll ask me to come back. So hopefully I won't be gone for long,' he said, trying to look on the positive side. 'And even though I won't be in the same house, I'll still be there for you, Izzy. You can call me anytime you like.'

Before he left, Malcolm helped me put together the scrapbook for Mum. I found an empty photo album at the back of one of the cabinets in the living room and started taking out photos from other albums to add to the scrapbook. The first photo I put in was one of me as a baby – I'd just been born and Mum was cradling me in her arms, a happy but exhausted smile on her face. I also put in another baby photo of me splashing about in my baby bath. I added a photo of me in a nativity play I did at primary school – I was five years old and was one of the Three Wise Men, bringing a gift of frankincense for the baby Jesus. Even though it was yonks ago, I can still remember the play really well. I had a fake beard that kept falling down and I was continually trying to fix it whilst trying to remember my lines at the same time. Luckily I had some help from my teacher Mrs McCurdy, who was whispering them to me from behind the stage. Next I put in a photo of me, Mum and Malcolm riding camels in Egypt, and then a photo of Mum in her office at work, and a photo of Auntie Rhona and Tofu.

Malcolm chose a photo of him and Mum dancing on the beach on our most recent holiday to Majorca, the two of them looking blissfully happy, along with a photo he took of me and Mum when we were doing a duet at the resort's karaoke night. Then he chose another photo of him and Mum ice-skating together. He also put in a love heart that he'd made out of a paper napkin on their very first date, which Mum had kept. I put in one of my baby booties – it did come as a pair, but years ago the other bootie got lost. I slipped it under the clear plastic but I had to stick the plastic down with lots of tape so that the bootie didn't fall out.

I collected some items from the cupboard under the stairs, which was mainly full of junk and other things Mum and Malcolm hadn't thrown out yet. One of those things was my very first baby tooth, which I found in an envelope in a box that had old toys in it. The tooth was all brown and scuzzy, but I still wanted Mum to see it because I know there was a time when it meant a lot to her. From the box I also took out a painting I did when I was little. It was a picture of me and Mum standing in front of the lion enclosure at Bristol Zoo. We both had stick-like arms and legs with wobbly red smiles on our faces. My lions didn't look too lion-y, though; they were just orangey blobs with white zigzag lines that were meant to be their teeth. But I can still remember the pride on my mum's face when I showed it to her. I folded it in half and put it in the scrapbook.

I found an article cut out from a newspaper – it was about Mum and her old colleagues at Thornley's Bank when they did a sixteen-hour sponsored line dance to raise money for the RSPCA. In the article there's a picture of Mum and her colleagues dressed up in cowboy and cowgirl outfits and they're all standing in a line with their cowboy hats held out to the camera. The last item that Malcolm put into the scrapbook were tickets to last year's FA Cup Final that he took Mum to. The tickets were originally Vince's, but he gave them to Malcolm after getting dumped by his girlfriend Eleanor a week before. He'd planned to take her to the game and thought going on his own would be too upsetting. It was the first time Mum had been to a football match and she'd really enjoyed it. The very last item I put into the scrapbook was a haiku I did in Year Six. It went:

Mum you are so kind
There is no one else like you
Thanks for everything.

I decorated the cover with drawings of daisies and butterflies and, using my red glitter pen, I wrote the words 'Mum's life'.

'Tell her I love her,' said Malcolm as he was about to go, his suitcase by his side.

'I don't want you to leave, Malcolm,' I bleated. 'Please don't abandon us. I need you here and so does Mum even though she doesn't know it.'

'I'm not abandoning you, Izzy, but your mum... she's not going to be able to handle me being here. That's why I have to go.'

'I'm really going to miss you,' I told him.

'And I'll miss you too. Bye, Izzy,' he said, kissing me on the cheek.

'Bye, Malcolm,' I murmured, watching him leave.

***

Three days later the doctors let Mum leave the hospital. They reckoned she was well enough to come home even though her amnesia hadn't gone away. While she was still in hospital, though, she allowed me to visit her again. She wasn't as rude to me as before but she was still insisting I call her Rio. She also told me that she was happy to be my friend which did make me feel quite hurt because I didn't want her to be my friend, I wanted her to be my mum. But then I also didn't want her to not talk to me so I really had no choice but to accept it.

Our chats were nice, though, and unlike before she did seem more interested in finding out all about me. I told her my favourite colour was fuchsia, my favourite TV show was *Neighbours* and my favourite musicians were Little Mix, Justin Timberlake and Demi Lovato. I let her listen to their music on my iPhone. She said she liked the songs but reckoned nineties music was much better than today's music. I told her that I wanted to be a singer when I grew up and she asked me to sing a song to hear how good my voice was. I did and she said I was very good. Plus I let her know all about my friends.

But Mum was keen to know more about the Internet and she listened in fascination as I explained online shopping to her. This didn't really come as any surprise to me, as she's loved online shopping for as long as I can remember.

'So the clothes are delivered to your house just the same as if you ordered them from a catalogue?' she said.

'Yes and you can get clothes delivered the very next day or food or books.'

'And what if you don't want the clothes?'

'You just send them back,' I said simply.

She was totally captivated by her Blackberry and couldn't stop playing with it when I gave it to her, taking lots of photos of the room. For a moment she reminded me of Alice, who'd recently got an iPhone like me and had literally been taking photos of everything.

'It's a camera and a phone, a phone and a camera, amazing!' Mum giggled, and I giggled too.

But then she got a little upset when she saw the names and numbers in the phone. She hardly recognised any of them. And she looked at me as though I was talking a foreign language when I tried to explain the ins and outs of our digital TV recorder and how it was possible to pause a live TV show and rewind it back.

But despite my explanation, Mum looked completely mystified. She couldn't get her head around a music download, either.

'So you can't pick it up like a CD or a cassette. You can't actually hold a download, is that right?'

'Yeah, that's right.'

'Weird,' she frowned.

However she did get excited when she sent what she thought was her first ever text message. She sent it to Grandad who'd gone off to get a cup of tea.

She wrote: Hi Dad, sys. I told her to put the 'sys' bit in and told her that it meant see you soon along with some other text-speak phrases like 'gr8' (great) and 'lol' (laugh out loud).

'It's like a whole new language,' she said, dazzled.

She read the newspapers Grandad brought in with him. She thought the world was very different from how it was back in 1995. She couldn't believe that Prince William was now a man and that she'd missed the Olympic Games coming to London and witnessing the Spice Girls become the biggest girl band of the late nineties.

Mum had a chat with Auntie Rhona on the phone. At first Mum didn't believe it was her because she said she sounded 'so grown up'. Then her voice went all wobbly as Auntie Rhona told Mum about her life in America. It was clear it was a lot for Mum to take in, she looked completely dumbfounded. Auntie Rhona told Mum other stuff too, like how the Tie-Dye Girls broke up once they went to college. She told Mum about the holiday they had in Crete to celebrate their twenty-first birthdays and the shopping spree they did in London when they got their first pay packets at their first proper jobs – Mum at the bank, Auntie Rhona at a design company. And she told Mum about the baby shower she threw for her when she was pregnant with me. Then they both giggled a bit when she told Mum that it was her who'd suggested the name 'Tofu' when Auntie Rhona had told her she'd bought a puppy and was also becoming a vegetarian. When Mum came off the phone, her eyes blinked rapidly.

'It was like Rhona was telling me about someone else, not me,' she said. 'I really am an adult.'

The evening before Mum came home I stuck Post-it notes around the house so she'd know where everything was kept. Karen, the therapist, had suggested

I do this – that way Mum might start to feel more comfortable in our home again. I stuck them on the cupboards in the kitchen so she'd know which ones had plates and cups in them and which ones had food. And I stuck them around the living room so she'd know which cabinet had CDs and DVDs in it, and which cabinet contained stuff like stamps and notepaper. And I put post-its on the doors upstairs, so she wouldn't get confused about which room was the bathroom and which was her bedroom. I did lots of tidying up too, to make the place look as nice as possible for her welcome home. Grandad helped out. He did all the vacuuming while I did all the dusting. Mum was always really particular about having a clean and tidy house, so I wanted it to be as nice as possible for her.

Both me and Grandad went to collect Mum on the day she was discharged. We took a taxi back to the house and on the journey Grandad and I were pointing out all the new shops and buildings to Mum.

'You see that Costa coffee shop over there, Rio, that's where the record shop used to be,' Grandad was telling her. 'And that mobile phone shop on your right, that was the old bookshop. The doctor's surgery's moved. It's further down the high street now. The old surgery building was converted into posh flats a few years back. Thornley's Bank is still next to it, though, where you used to work. And the old chip shop is still there, Thank Cod, which we're just coming to now. There used to be another chip shop further down the high street, but that's now a chicken shop called Texas Chicken King.'

'Who do delicious spicy chicken wings,' I added.

'The library is still at the other end of the high street along with the post office,' said Grandad.

But Mum didn't say a word to either of us as she gazed out the window. She was looking at everything – the new shops, people talking on their phones, people with shopping bags, other cars going past, and she looked amazed by all of it.

'And this is where you live,' said Grandad when the taxi pulled up outside our house.

'Why don't we live in our house any more, Dad?' said Mum as we got out the car. Her face looked terrified. 'I want to go back to our house.'

'I sold that house years ago, Rio. I live in a little flat, which is just a couple of streets away,' said Grandad, trying to smile, but looking worried. 'This is your house, you own it.'

He took hold of Mum's hand as if she was a little

girl and we walked slowly up the path.

'Don't be scared, Rio, the house isn't going to bite,' Grandad whispered to her.

As we went in Mum's eyes were scanning everywhere – the coat stand, the staircase, the sofa, the framed photos on the mantelpiece, the books on the bookshelves, the Post-it notes I'd put on the cabinets. She rubbed her arms as if the house was freezing cold.

'Don't worry, sweetheart, you'll get to know this place again,' said Grandad, which for a moment made me worry that maybe she wouldn't and would be stuck never being able to remember how her life was beyond the age of fourteen.

'Would you like to watch some telly?' I asked her.

She shrugged but then went up to the TV.

'How come this telly's so thin? It doesn't look like the telly we had, Dad.'

'That's because it's a plasma TV,' said Grandad. 'They're all the rage now, y'know.'

'And what's that black box underneath it?'

'That's the digital recorder I was telling you about,' I said.

'But what if I want to watch a film; do we have a video player?'

'People don't really watch videos any more, sweetheart,' said Grandad.

'We watch DVDs or Blu-ray discs, or download films. We've got loads of DVD films in the cabinet and this TV has an inbuilt DVD player,' I said, opening the DVD slot to show her.

'By the way, I thought I'd order us a takeaway tonight,' said Grandad. 'Do you fancy some take-away sushi, Rio?'

'Sushi? Isn't that raw fish?' said Mum.

'Not all of it is raw, but sushi's your favourite food, Rio,' I said.

It still felt odd calling my mum by her name.

'It is?' she said, making a face. 'No, I don't want to have it. I don't want any sushi.'

'Well, why don't I get us all a Chinese instead,' said Grandad. 'Do you fancy Chinese, Rio?'

'OK,' she mouthed, her arms wrapped around her.

I switched on the TV. *Coronation Street* was on and right away it grabbed Mum's attention. Grandad and I watched it with her, me sitting in the armchair opposite and Grandad sitting with Mum on the sofa, but we'd already missed most of it and soon the programme was over.

'I used to watch *Coronation Street* all the

time, but I didn't recognise any of the characters except for that woman with the short hair and she looks really old now. It's all so different,' Mum moaned.

'It would be, Rio,' said Grandad. 'The programme's had countless characters since you were fourteen.'

As soon as our takeaway arrived, Grandad and I couldn't wait to tuck in but Mum mostly picked at the food, her eyes constantly darting round the kitchen before she suddenly got up and went over to the fridge. On the door were loads of magnets that she'd collected over the years, many bought on holidays we'd been on. There was one that was in the design of a Californian number plate and it had the words San Diego written on it. Mum had bought it when we went to visit Auntie Rhona a few years ago. There was another magnet that was in the shape of pyramids that she got on our holiday in Egypt and another that had a picture of a palm tree on it with 'Barbados' written underneath. Mum ran her fingers over the magnets, her eyes staring at them inquisitively. She pulled one of them off, the magnet from Barbados.

'Have I been here?' she asked.

'Uh-huh. We went on holiday there five years ago,' I said.

'Which was just before you met—' Grandad was about to say Malcolm's name but stopped himself.

'Before you met Malcolm,' I said. I didn't want to upset Mum, but I wasn't prepared to act like Malcolm didn't exist, especially as the place felt so empty without him.

Mum put the magnet back on the fridge. 'I'm going to go and watch some more telly,' she said, then wandered out of the kitchen.

'She's really changed, Grandad,' I said glumly. 'One minute she's quiet and looks really sad, then the next minute it's like she's ready to bite my head off.'

'She's probably feeling a mixture of emotions right now, Izzy,' he replied. 'You would too if you found yourself transported to almost two decades into the future. Your mum's forgotten half her life, sweetheart, and I imagine it's going to take her some time to adjust.'

'Maybe I should give her the scrapbook; that might cheer her up.'

I went upstairs to grab it from my room and came back down to give it to Mum. She was lying on the sofa, her legs curled up to her chest, her head on the armrest. The TV was on but she wasn't watching it. She was just staring into space like a lost little girl. I couldn't get used to seeing her like this – it was as though someone else had been transplanted into my mum's body. I'd do anything to help her get her memories back.

'Rio, I have something to show you,' I said to her.

'What is it?' she mumbled.

I put the scrapbook in front of her and gradually she sat up.

'It's to help you remember,' I said as she turned to the first page that had the photo of her holding me as a baby.

'That's me,' she muttered, blinking.

'And that's me,' I said. 'I was only a few days old.'

She turned to the next page where there was a photo of her cosied up with Malcolm.

'It's that man,' she said sourly.

'Well, he is a big part of our lives.'

'Your life, maybe, but not mine,' she replied harshly.

She turned the page again to a photo of her sitting at her desk at work, typing away at the computer. She was wearing a light-grey suit.

'Your boss Victoria took that one.'

'I look like a business woman,' she said before turning the page to the picture I'd painted of the two of us at Bristol Zoo. She unfolded it and took a look.

'You really loved this picture,' I said to her. 'It was on the fridge door for ages.'

Then she looked at the photo of Auntie Rhona and Tofu.

'Rhona looks like a business woman too.'

Then suddenly she slammed the book shut and chucked it to the floor. 'Why did you have to show me this?' she started to rage. 'I hate that I can't remember any of it. I don't know that life, Izzy!'

She fled the room, running upstairs.

'What's happened?' said Grandad, coming out of the kitchen.

'It's the scrapbook, Grandad,' I croaked, tears stinging my eyes. 'It didn't work.'

Eleven

The next day before school I woke up earlier than usual and headed downstairs to make my mum some breakfast. I wanted to make it up to her for upsetting her with the scrapbook. I boiled her an egg and made her some toast with marmalade. I put it on a tray and took it up to her. When I knocked on her bedroom door, she was still asleep so I quietly crept in and woke her up.

'Rio, I've made you some breakfast,' I whispered.

'What time is it?' she mumbled sleepily.

I showed her my watch.

'Are you crazy? Just go away!' she scowled and dived under the covers.

I wondered to myself if this is what it would be like to have an older sister, always having a go at me. I knew it was like that for Holly, who was always getting into arguments with her sister Violet. I put the tray on her dressing table in case she changed her mind and went back downstairs. After making myself a bowl of cornflakes I got changed into my uniform, then grabbed my bag and left for school. When I arrived, Alice and Holly were practising the dance routine for the party while Layla was sitting on our bench.

'Hi, Iz,' said my friends, greeting me.

'You must be so glad your mum's back home,' said Layla.

I swallowed. 'Yeah, I'm . . . really happy,' I said to them, putting on my cheeriest smile.

I wish I could've been brave enough to tell them that my mum had amnesia and that she and Malcolm were no longer a couple, but I just couldn't seem to find the words to explain it to them. Besides, all my friends wanted to talk about was Layla's party.

During maths, Layla filled me in on the latest party news. She had to whisper it though as Mr

Carling, our maths teacher, didn't like people talking in class unless it was when we had our hands up with a question. She told me that as well as a candy floss machine and a chocolate fountain, she was also planning to have a hot dog stall, and an Xbox for people to play FIFA on. And there would be a 'chill-out zone' for people to relax in. It did sound really exciting, but as she was telling me everything I did feel a little downhearted that my life wasn't as fun and as happy right now as Layla's was.

At break Holly wanted to know if I'd decided on an outfit to wear to the party. When I told her I wasn't sure what I was going to wear, she waggled her finger at me like Mr Carling does whenever we get the wrong answer to a maths question.

'You'll have to make a decision soon, Izzy,' she said. 'Layla's party is less than two weeks away.'

At lunch time we had another rehearsal behind the art block. Holly was finally doing the dance moves correctly, much to Layla's delight.

'I think we danced really well today,' she said as we came together for a group hug.

When the bell went we quickly gathered up our things and, as we began to walk to our next class, I heard someone call my name. It was Sam; his brown eyes meeting with mine, making my stomach flutter. But it was Layla he wanted to speak to.

'Is it true you've booked Master Slick to DJ at your party?' he asked her.

'Yeah, it's true,' she replied with a grin.

'Quality!' said Sam. 'I've listened to some of his mixes on YouTube; he's a wicked DJ.' He turned to me. 'How's your mum doing?' he asked, which my friends took as their cue to leave.

'Laters,' said Alice, giving me a quick nudge.

'We'll see you in class,' said Layla, giving me a knowing wink.

I suddenly felt seriously shy being alone with Sam.

'My mum's home now,' I said to him, the palms of my hands feeling warm with nerves.

'Great. That's really good news,' he said. 'I hear you're singing at Layla's party with the others.'

'Yeah . . . we're gonna dress up as Little Mix and sing their song "Wings".'

'Nice. So do you like singing then?'

I nodded. 'I want be a pop star when I'm older.'

'Cool. I'm planning to be a vet. I love animals.'

'Me too, but I'm allergic to most of them. I could never own a cat or a dog.'

'I don't have any allergies, but I do I have a dog, a German shepherd. He's called Barney.'

'That's a sweet name.'

'Yeah, I know. He's three years old. We got him as a puppy from a rescue centre. We're still training him 'cos he can be a bit naughty sometimes, especially when me and my brother Tom are playing a game of football. Barney's always trying to grab the ball and run off with it. And when it comes to food, he can be a proper greedy guts. At tea time, he always tries to jump up and steal the food off mine and Tom's plates.'

I giggled.

'Oi, are you coming to our PE lesson, or what?' Sam's friend Enzo called, approaching us and throwing a ball into Sam's hands.

'Yeah, I'm coming,' he said. 'See you round, Izzy.'

It had been nice talking to Sam again and finding out a bit more about him; I liked him even more.

Mum was in a better mood when I got home compared to the previous night. Grandad was taking her through the scrapbook, and instead of throwing it on the floor she listened with interest as he told her about the photos and the other things that were in it. She also apologised to me.

'I'm sorry I was a bit sharp with you yesterday,' she said. 'Seeing all those pictures of myself, well, it was a big shock. I know I'm supposed to be an adult, but I just don't feel like one. My dad showed me my wedding dress today; I can't believe I was really going to get married. It's like my whole life has just fast forwarded, but I've not been there to see it all happen.'

'We understand, Rio,' said Grandad, patting Mum's knee. 'You won't have to deal with this on your own. We'll help you fill in the blanks.'

'Yeah, we'll tell you everything you need to know,' I said.

Grandad rang Karen, the therapist, and she just told him that we'd have to be patient and try to keep Mum as calm as we could – hopefully that way her memories would come back naturally.

As the week went by, Grandad and I helped Mum settle in as best we could and helped her learn more about the life she'd forgotten. I showed her how to make her own recipe of Thai green curry and got her to help me chop the chicken while I made the paste and boiled the rice. It did feel strange telling my mum how to cook something she'd taught me how to do. I felt the same when I showed her how to use the washing machine, which she couldn't figure out how to operate. Grandad explained how to send an email and how to scan a photo then print it.

On Saturday me and Grandad took Mum around the town. It was like we were tourists as we took her to the local landmarks. She said the library hadn't changed a bit. We took her to the community centre where Layla was going to be holding her party. There was a yoga class on – Mum couldn't believe it when I told her she'd been going to yoga for a few months and was quite good at it. And we showed her the art gallery on the high street where we would often go to check out the latest exhibit-ions. Afterwards we went to see Kye at the salon. I'd called him the day before to let him know we'd be stopping by. He already knew about Mum's amnesia. Mum's boss Victoria told him as he does her hair as well.

'Izzy says you're my hairdresser,' said Mum to Kye.

'Yes, I am,' he replied pleasantly. 'You come in about every two months to see me for a trim. Izzy probably told you it was me who put in your extensions. You were so happy that day. You couldn't wait to marry Malcolm.'

'I can't believe I could ever have been happy about marrying that hideous man,' said Mum, looking appalled.

Kye didn't have a clue how to respond to this remark. I couldn't bear hearing my mum insult Malcolm in that way, but I told myself it was because she'd forgotten how much she loved him. We didn't stay long at the salon.

We finished our afternoon at Café Olé.

'So do we come here a lot?' Mum wanted to know.

'Yes, it's our favourite place,' I said as we drank cappuccinos. 'You've been bringing me here ever since I was little.'

'It sounds like we do a lot of stuff together. Have we always been very close?' she asked me awkwardly.

'Yeah. Although you can be a little bossy sometimes, you're always nagging me about putting out the bins and putting the toothpaste top back on,' I laughed.

Mum laughed too. 'You always nag me to do the same, don't you, Dad?'

'Yes, and I could never get you to do any of it.'

'I think it's nice that we're close,' said Mum to me, which made me smile.

Overall it had been a nice day and it felt like Mum had finally accepted that she wasn't a teenager, even though none of her memories had come back yet. Plus we were getting on much better. I'd have to get used to being just friends for a bit.

On Monday when I got home from school Grandad was reading a newspaper on the sofa.

'Where's Mum?' I asked him, putting down my school bag.

'Upstairs.'

'And how has she been?'

'She did get a bit upset earlier when Belinda and Kevin came round. She couldn't believe how much they'd both changed. Kevin is six years younger than your mum and she only remembers him as a boy, so she was shocked to see that he's now a grown man. They did speak about the old days, though, which I think she enjoyed and they both told her about their lives now. Anyway, we went to see her GP who's given her a certificate signing her off work, which means she won't have to go back until she's ready.'

I went upstairs to get changed out of my uniform. Mum was in my bedroom going through my wardrobe. I couldn't believe it. Worse, she was wearing my orange ra-ra skirt from Forever 21 and one of my vests that made her boobs look squashy and massive. I was gobsmacked.

'What are you doing wearing my clothes?' I said, aghast.

'Sorry,' she said in a voice that didn't sound at all apologetic, 'I should've really asked you first.'

'But you have lots of nice clothes in your own wardrobe. Why do you want to wear mine?'

Mum made a face. 'My clothes are ugly. It's like I've become someone with no style. I might just take those clothes to a charity shop.'

'You can't do that!' I exclaimed. 'You love your clothes and a lot of them are designer outfits.'

'Love those clothes? You must be joking,' she replied flatly.

She pulled out my grey zipped leather jacket.

'That's not going to fit you,' I said to her, but she

tried it on anyway.

The jacket came up tight on her; she could just about move her arms. She looked like the Tin Man in *The Wizard of Oz*, the jacket creaking when she moved.

'Do you mind if I borrow these clothes for a while?' she said, twirling in front of the wardrobe mirror.

I grimaced. 'I don't think they suit you.'

'Yes, they do! They look great on me,' she argued.

'Seriously, Rio, they don't and I'm not saying that to be horrible.'

'I can't believe how selfish you're being, Izzy. Has no one ever told you that it's good to share?'

'But you're too old to be wearing my clothes.'

'I'm only borrowing them. It'll just be for a few days,' she said, pulling the same type of pout I do when I want something.

I really didn't want her wearing my clothes, but I also didn't want to see her unhappy.

'All right, you can borrow them, but it's just this one time, OK?'

'Thanks,' she replied and sauntered off downstairs.

Grandad was just as horrified when he saw Mum in my clothes.

'Rio, why on earth are you wearing Izzy's clothes?' he asked her.

''Cos they look nice on me,' she said simply.

'No, they don't, you look silly in them,' said Grandad, shaking out his newspaper in annoyance.

'Well, I'm not going to stop you from having an opinion, Dad, but personally I think I look great. And can you stop looking at me like I've just robbed a bank. They're only clothes, Dad. Jeez,' said Mum huffily.

'When are you going to realise, Rio, you're not a young person any more. You're thirty-three years old!' said Grandad. 'I know you don't remember that but you only have to look in mirror to see that it's not a fourteen-year-old looking back at you.'

'But I don't feel thirty-three,' said Mum. 'I still feel like the girl who used to eat lemon sherbets with Rhona in the park and spend her Saturday afternoons browsing through CDs in the record shop, or in the chippie playing *Street Fighter* on the arcade machine. I want to listen to Kenny Kennedy on my Walkman on the way to school and look forward to getting my copy of the latest *Smash Hits* magazine so I can tear out the posters of him and put them on my wall. That girl . . . I'm still her and that's why I need your help.'

'What kind of help?' I asked.

'I need you to help me fulfil a wish. I want to sing a duet with Kenny Kennedy. I'd like you to help me find him.'

Twelve

'You want to find Kenny Kennedy,' I said, perplexed. 'Why? That's so random.'

'And why on earth do you want to do a duet with him?' said Grandad.

'Because he promised to do a duet with me and it's all I can think about,' said Mum.

'Did he? When?' asked Grandad.

'When Rhona and me snuck into his dressing room at his concert. It feels like just last month to me, even though I know it was years ago. We sang one of our songs to him, and he told us he'd like to do a duet with us one day.'

'He was lying to you, Rio. He probably just said that to get you and Rhona out of his dressing room. I doubt he meant a word of it,' said Grandad in Portuguese, shaking his head.

'He did mean it,' Mum insisted. 'He probably just lost my number.'

I pulled a face. 'But Kenny doesn't sing any more.'

'He might do it one last time.'

'But how are you even going to get hold him?' Grandad continued in Portuguese. 'As Izzy said, he's not a pop star any more, Rio.'

'Well, maybe I could find him through that googi . . . goggle website or whatever it's called.'

'Google,' I corrected her.

'So will you help me find him, Izzy?' said Mum, looking at me in earnest. 'Doing the duet would make me really happy.'

Reluctantly I agreed to help her. After dinner, I went to my room and called Malcolm on my mobile. It was so good to hear his voice. I told him about school (how boring it was) and how my rehearsals were going for Layla's party. And of course I told him about Mum wanting to find Kenny Kennedy.

I thought he'd say it was a barmy idea us trying to

find him, but he actually thought it was a good thing.

'I didn't realise she was such a huge fan, but perhaps if she meets Kenny and sees how he's now a middle-aged man maybe it'll help her come to terms with the fact that she's not young, either,' he said.

'Do you reckon?'

'Yes, I think it could be quite good for her.'

But I was still a little sceptical, especially as I didn't know how we were going to find him. I asked Malcolm if he had any ideas.

'A few months ago your mum was reading one of the supplement magazines from a newspaper and there was an article about Kenny and some other faded pop stars. It was one of those "Where are they now?" type of articles. At the time I didn't realise how much she liked him – perhaps she'd even forgotten herself. Anyway I distinctly remember her telling me how he was now a manager of a coffee shop in London, which I know really surprised her. I guess she thought he'd be living it up on the French Riviera or somewhere like that, enjoying his millions. The coffee shop had a funny name. Beany...Beans and Buns...no, Beans and Baps, that was it, and, oh yeah, he was also going by the name of Charlie Kennedy, his real name. Kenny Kennedy was just a stage name. '

'That's great, thanks, Malcolm.'

I was about to put down the phone when Malcolm stopped me and asked his usual question.

'Does she remember me?'

I didn't want to tell him, but it was only right that I told him the truth.

'No, she doesn't,' I muttered, which made him go quiet for a minute.

'And her memories, have any of them come back?' he asked.

'No, she still can't remember anything beyond the age of fourteen.' I sighed, and Malcolm sighed too.

'I miss her so much, Izzy. I miss the both of you,' he said, his voice turning sad. 'Anyway, I'll speak to you soon.'

After I'd come off the phone, I looked up Beans and Baps on the Internet and scribbled down the address and telephone number that came up on Google. I then called the number. After a few rings someone picked up.

'Beans and Baps, how may I help?' said the voice at the other end.

'Can I speak to Charlie Kennedy, please?'

'Yes, Charlie speaking.'

I hung up and ran downstairs.

Mum and Grandad were watching the telly.

'I've found him,' I bellowed. 'I've found Kenny Kennedy.'

'I honestly thought it would take you a lot longer to find him,' said Grandad as he used his credit card to book mine and Mum's train tickets to London. I had a school inset day on Friday, so we'd be going then. 'But I wonder what he's doing running a coffee shop in London? I'd thought an ex-pop star like him would be living somewhere more glamorous, like the Hollywood Hills.'

'Maybe he fancied a new career,' said Mum.

'Or squandered most of his money, more like,' said Grandad.

'Well, whatever he did with his money, I don't care. I'm so looking forward to seeing him and doing the duet.'

'Rio,' I said to Mum steadily, 'I know you're dying to do this duet, but there is a chance he might not want to do it, y'know.'

'Yes he will, 'cos I'm his biggest fan,' said Mum, reminding me of Layla for a second, who was always going on about Chase Dooley.

'But from the sounds of it, Rio, he's retired from singing. He wouldn't be running a coffee shop otherwise,' said Grandad.

But Mum had a determined look on her face – she seemed convinced that the duet would happen. For her sake I hoped it would.

Thirteen

I woke up late on Friday after forgetting to set my alarm clock. Me and Mum were due to get the ten-forty train to London. She'd woken up late too, and after a very quick breakfast I phoned for a taxi to take us to the station. When the taxi arrived, I popped my head round Mum's bedroom door to check that she was all changed and ready, but I was stunned to see she was wearing another one of my tops. It was a yellow T-shirt that had a picture of a pink flamingo on it. It was one of my favourite tops and I just couldn't believe she'd gone and raided my wardrobe again.

'I hope you don't mind me borrowing this,' she said.

I was reeling, but I didn't want to get into an argument over it right then.

'No, I don't mind,' I mumbled.

As soon as we got to the station and on the train, Mum fell asleep. But half an hour later she woke up wanting to know if we were in London yet.

'We have another hour to go before we get there,' I told her, which made her roll her eyes.

'You would've thought someone would've invented a train that could travel at lightning speed. I always thought the future would be all hi-tech but it's kinda boring except for that phone of mine that's also a camera. 2014 is so dull. What do you even call this stupid decade?'

I shrugged. 'Um ... I'm not sure ... the tens or maybe the tenties.'

'The tenties! What a silly name,' said Mum. Then she smiled to herself. 'I wonder what Kenny looks like now. I wonder if his hair is still in that spiky style. Nearly every girl at Broomwood was in love with him and wished Kenny was their boyfriend.' She looked at me wryly. 'Do you have a boyfriend, Izzy?'

I shook my head. 'No.'

'Is there someone you fancy then?'

'No,' I said again quickly. Even though my answer wasn't true, I wondered why she was asking me this.

'Yes there is, I can tell,' said Mum, her lips curving into a smile.

But then I thought that maybe I should just tell her about Sam. Before my mum's accident I wouldn't have dared to tell her in case she'd have said I was too young to be thinking about a boyfriend, but I guessed she would react differently now.

'OK, there is someone. His name is Sam and he's in my French class at school.'

'Sammmm,' she purred. 'And is he cute?'

'Very,' I gushed as I began to tell Mum more about him.

'He sounds nice,' she said once I'd told her everything.

'My friend Layla reckons I should just tell Sam that I like him, but I'm way too shy to do that.'

'You could always invite him out on a date but make out that it's not a date,' Mum suggested. 'You could ask him to help you with your French homework, but the both of you go to McDonald's to do it. That's what I'd do.'

'I guess I could do that but, like I said, I'm just too shy so maybe I'll wait for him to ask me out first.'

'Well, it's up to you but I know what I would do if I were in your situation and I definitely wouldn't be waiting for him to ask me out.'

I was quite surprised – Mum told me she'd never had a boyfriend until she met my dad when she was twenty. I couldn't work out whether Mum had been telling me white lies to make sure I behaved, or whether Rio's confidence was all talk.

When the train arrived in London we got a taxi outside the station and asked the driver to take us straight to Beans and Baps, which was in the heart of London's West End.

Mum didn't say much. She was nibbling away at her nails, and when we got out of the taxi, I noticed her hands were trembling.

'We're here.' I looked at Mum with concern. 'Are you OK, Rio?'

'Yeah, I'm fine, let's go and see Kenny,' she said,

but as we stood outside the café, Mum began to have second thoughts. 'Actually, I'm not sure I'm quite ready to face him yet. I think I need to psych myself up first.'

'OK . . . we can go somewhere else then. Over there, maybe?' I said pointing at another café called Marano's on the opposite side. 'We could get something to eat first then go back over.'

Mum nodded and we both wandered over to the other side of the road and went into the café. I ordered two tuna and mozzarella paninis. Mum was curious to find out what a panini sandwich tasted like; she didn't think she'd ever had one before. She also wanted a Cherry Coke, telling the waitress it was her favourite drink, but they didn't have any so she just ordered an ordinary Coke.

'Cherry Coke's not actually your favourite drink,' I said to Mum after the waitress had taken our order. 'You like sparkling water. You always have that whenever we go out for a meal.'

'I like water best? Eurgh,' she guffawed. 'I've seriously become so uncool.' She began to bite her fingernails again.

'Are you sure you're OK?' I asked her.

'I suppose I'm just a little nervous about meeting Kenny. He is my idol, after all, and I'm not sure what I'm actually going to say to him.'

'Why don't you just tell Kenny you were once a fan of his?'

'*Am* a fan, not *was*, am,' Mum corrected me.

The waitress brought over our paninis and drinks.

'OK, well, just say you're still a fan and ask him if he'd be interested in doing a duet with you 'cos that is why we're here.'

'You're right, it's probably best to just come out with it, even though I haven't actually thought about where we're going to do this duet. If Kenny's not singing any more then he might not have a studio we can go to.'

'Maybe he won't mind the two of you singing together in the café. I could record it on my phone so you'll have a video of it.'

'Yeah, that'd be so orbital.'

'*So orbital*? What does that mean?'

'Oh, it's just something me and Rhona like to say. Or used to say. It means fantastic.'

Mum bit into her panini, her head bobbing from side to side as she chewed. 'It tastes really good,' she said. 'I wish my school served food like this in the nineties instead of that disgusting shepherd's pie they were always giving us. Is Broomwood still doing shepherd's pie for lunch?'

'Yep, every Wednesday, and it's still disgusting,' I said, creasing up with laughter. Mum laughed too, and for a moment it was just like how it used to be between us.

When we'd finished our paninis, Mum paid the bill with Grandad's credit card. He'd given it to her for the day as she couldn't remember the pin number for her own. We then went back over to Beans and Baps.

'Hi, we're looking for Kenny?' said Mum to the waiter that approached us.

'She means Charlie,' I quickly corrected as the waiter raised a curious eyebrow. 'We're looking for Charlie Kennedy.'

'I'm sorry but Charlie's not in yet. He normally comes in at about half three on a Friday,' said the waiter in an Australian accent.

I checked my watch. It was a quarter past one.

'We've got ages yet until he comes in. What do you want to do, Rio?' I asked Mum.

'I guess we could do some shopping seeing as I've got this with me,' she said, waving the credit card. 'Let's go to Oxford Street.'

'Grandad gave that to you to buy food, not clothes. I don't think you should be spending any more money on it.'

'Gosh, you're a right misery pants, aren't you? You need to learn to chill out, Izzy. Anyway, I wasn't planning to spend lots of money on it, just a little, that's all.'

I couldn't believe my mum would ever think of spending Grandad's money without asking him. The image of her as a teenager that I'd pieced together was suddenly falling apart.

When we got to Oxford Street, spending 'a little' appeared to be the last thing on Mum's mind.

'I'm gonna buy this and this . . . and this as well,' she sang as she went through Topshop, picking out tons of clothes and throwing them over her arm. And when they became too heavy to carry she offloaded some onto me; the two of us plodding like penguins to the fitting room. I waited for her as she tried them on.

'How do I look?' said Mum, stepping out of the cubicle in her first outfit. She had on a zebra-striped onesie which, if it wasn't for her amnesia, there's no way she'd be seen dead in.

'Yeah, it's . . . nice,' I fibbed, 'but maybe you should try on something else.'

Unfortunately the other clothes she tried on didn't suit her, either; they just looked too young for her. The only outfit that did suit her was a blue dress, which I managed to persuade her to buy over all the other clothes she'd brought to the fitting room.

We went into H&M next and I decided to find something to wear to Layla's party tomorrow. As I was planning to look like Jade from Little Mix, I needed to find something in her style. A pink chiffon blouse immediately caught my eye and I decided to buy it along with a pair of black shorts. I also got a white crop top that had the words 'Gonna Be Famous' written across it and a pair of denim shorts. Mum bought a pair of pink sandals and a pair of leopard print pumps.

'So are you looking forward to your friend's party?' Mum asked.

'Yeah, I can't wait, but there is a bit of me that's nervous about our performance. I've never sung in front of an audience before,' I replied, then suddenly thought about the song I'd planned to sing at Mum's wedding and how that was supposed to be my first time in front of an audience.

'You'll be fine, Izzy,' Mum said. When we got to the checkout, she added, 'If you want I'll pay for your stuff.'

'No, it's OK, I'll use my own money,' I said and gave the shop assistant my debit card.

'How come you've got a card? You don't work,' said Mum when we left the shop. 'I never had a card when I was at school. I didn't even have a bank account.'

'Well, lots of kids have bank accounts now,' I told her. 'You and Malcolm normally put money into my account, but I always make sure I spend the money wisely, something you're very strict about.'

Mum wanted to go to Selfridges next and I had my fingers crossed she wouldn't spend any more on Grandad's card. She wanted to look at their handbags, and as we wandered round I tried reminding her that she had plenty of handbags at home in the hope it would put her off from buying another one.

'Did I come here for the January sales?' she said suddenly. 'I remember standing in this exact same spot and I'm sure you were there with me. You had your hair in a ponytail and I think you were wearing a red skirt.'

I gaped at her in amazement. 'You remember.'

It felt like all my birthdays and Christmases had come at once. My mum's memory was finally coming back; it was the best news ever. I felt so full of emotion that my eyes immediately began to fill with tears but they were tears of joy.

'I think I remember,' said Mum, but with a quizzical look on her face. 'I bought a bag that day.'

'Yeah, you did. I'm so glad you can remember. You bought your blue Mulberry bag. Is there anything else you can remember?' I said as I wiped my eyes with the back of my hand, my heart beating with anticipation.

'I love buying things in the sales, don't I?' said Mum.

I smiled. 'Uh-huh. You like it when you can get a discount on things. Do you remember anything else about that day – like the other shops we went to or the other stuff you bought?'

'It's very hazy,' she said, rubbing the side of her head with her fingers. 'Did we . . . erm . . . go to French Connection?'

'Yes!'

'I bought a couple of tops.'

I nodded excitedly. 'But we went to other shops too. Can you remember which ones they were?' I pressed.

She squeezed her eyes together as she tried to think. But then she sighed. 'Nothing more is coming.'

'Well, do you remember other things like when you taught me how to swim and all the birthday cards and Mother's Day cards I used to make for you? And do you remember all our holidays? Like when we went to Egypt – we visited the Great Pyramids and Malcolm got all petrified when we went camel riding. Do you remember your life with Malcolm?' I said all in a rush.

'No, I don't remember,' she replied, which made my heart sink a little.

'OK, well it's still really good that your memories are coming back.'

'Yeah, it is good,' said Mum, but her face looked more worried than pleased about this. 'Can we go now? Kenny will be arriving at the café soon,' she said hastily.

I checked my watch. It was twenty past three.

Despite Mum's sudden moodiness I was really happy that she'd been able to remember a few things at last. I couldn't wait to tell Grandad and Malcolm.

'Hello again,' said the Australian waiter when we returned to Beans and Baps. 'Charlie's still not here yet, but you're welcome to wait. Can I get you anything to eat or drink?'

Mum ordered a Cherry Coke, which this café had, plus a slice of chocolate cake and I asked for a Sprite and a slice of carrot cake.

'I can't make up my mind which song to do with Kenny,' said Mum after the waiter had gone to get our cakes and drinks. 'I can't decide between his songs "Who Will It Be" and "Never Felt This Way".'

'Well, which of the songs do you like the best?'

'I like them both.'

'All right, why don't you just sing... "Who Will It Be",' I said to her, not that I'd actually heard of the song. Then I paused for a moment. 'Rio, I was just thinking that if Kenny isn't up for the duet, then there's nothing stopping us from doing the song together. You won't remember, but we did a karaoke duet when we went on holiday to Majorca. We sang "Forever" by this singer called Luna Abrahams.'

'I've never heard of her and I don't know why you're saying Kenny won't do the duet. He will, I'm sure of it.'

'I just said that in case he tells you that he can't,' I said. 'Luna Abrahams is a singer that you like. "Forever" is a really nice song, it came out a couple of years ago. It goes like this: *Our love is forever and we'll always be together. So find your way back.*'

'*To me, honey*,' Mum sang.

'Oh, my gosh, you remember the lyrics!' I said, my mouth open wide. 'Your memory really is coming back.'

'It was like the words just popped into my head,' said Mum.

'There's another song of hers that you like called "Timeless",' I said quickly.

I started singing the chorus to her and to my astonishment Mum was able to join in. She could remember nearly every lyric of the song. I felt so happy.

'That was so weird,' she said after we'd stopped singing. 'I've never heard of Luna Abrahams, but in my head I could remember what the song sounded like – and those lyrics, it was like they were there as well. I just knew them.' She looked totally amazed at herself.

'Well, hopefully this means the rest of your memories will start coming back now.'

At that moment a man walked into the café.

'Hello, Charlie,' said the Australian waiter from the counter.

Mum's jaw dropped to the table.

'He's here,' she whispered, her face glowing.

'How's the place been today?' said Kenny/Charlie to the waiter.

'A little quieter than usual. I imagine most people are in the park enjoying the sunshine,' said the waiter. 'By the way, you've got two visitors over there.'

He pointed towards us before disappearing through a door at the back of the café.

Kenny/Charlie turned round and straightaway I thought he looked nothing like the guy in the photos I'd seen on Google Images. For a start, his spiky brown hair was no longer spiky, instead it was completely grey with a bald patch in the middle, and the smooth clear skin he used to have was now lined and blotchy. He had a bushy beard that made him look slightly wild. He came over. 'Hello, can I help you?' he asked.

'K-K Ken . . .' Mum stuttered.

'You're Charlie, aren't you?' I stepped in.

'Yes, I'm Charlie. And you are?'

'Izzy and this is . . . Rio,' I said.

His eyebrows furrowed.

Mum stood up, her face looking slightly pained as though she'd just eaten something unpleasant.

'You look so old,' she mumbled.

'And am I supposed to take that as a compliment?' said Kenny/Charlie, suddenly looking irritated. 'So, who are you again?'

I looked at Mum. 'Go on, tell him.'

'I . . . I can't,' she murmured.

'Rio met you when she was a lot younger. It was backstage at one of your concerts in Birmingham. She was with her friend Rhona,' I told him.

'Oh yeah, and where's this story going?' he said warily.

'They both sang a song for you that they'd written themselves and you promised Rio and Rhona that you'd do a duet with them one day. So that's why we're here, so you can do the duet with Rio.'

'Look, kid, I don't make promises and furthermore I stopped being a singer many years ago. So I'm afraid I won't be doing any duet.' He walked back to the counter.

'Oh, please will you do it?' I pleaded, rushing up to him. 'We travelled miles on the train so Rio could get the chance to sing with you. It would mean—'

'Stop, Izzy. Just stop!' Mum shouted from the table. 'I don't want to do the duet with him. He's not Kenny!'

She ran out of the café. I quickly paid for our drinks and cakes, then rushed out after her.

'It is him,' I said. 'He might be calling himself Charlie, but he's definitely Kenny Kennedy.'

'I know it's him!' she snapped, swinging her shopping bags as she stood on the pavement.

'Well, if you know it's him, why did you just say that he wasn't? And why have you changed your mind about doing the duet?'

'Because he's not how I remember him. He's all . . . middle-aged,' she wailed. 'I want to sing with the Kenny who was in the posters on my wall: the Kenny who was absolutely gorgeous, not that wrinkly old man.'

'Surely you realised he was going to be older now. But he is the same person so let's just go back inside and I'll ask him again.'

'No. I don't want to do the duet any more,' said Mum angrily. 'I wish we'd never come to London. Why did you let me come here?'

'Me? This was your idea! You wanted to see him.'

'Well, you should've talked me out of coming. Why didn't you?'

''Cos you were desperate for us to come here, that's why. And I thought you seeing Kenny would finally make you realise that you're not a teenager, Mum.'

'I told you not to call me that. Don't you ever call me Mum!'

'But you *are* my mum. When are you going to accept that?'

'Never!' she yelled and burst into tears. 'Oh, why can't it just be 1995! Everything made sense then. I knew who I was. But right now I just feel like I'm stuck in the wrong body, in the wrong time. I just want to be fourteen again.'

'But you shouldn't have to feel like that. Especially now that your memories are coming back.' I tried to comfort her, but she batted my hand away.

'Leave me alone,' she shouted.

A knot of sadness formed in my throat. I actually felt like crying myself. It was like my mum was rejecting me all over again, just like she did when she awoke from the coma, and as we took a taxi back to the train station, I felt really down.

We didn't speak on the train journey back, and when we got home Mum went straight up to her room, slamming the door behind her.

'What's wrong with your mum?' asked Grandad as I lumbered into the living room. 'Didn't she get to meet Kenny?'

I joined him on the sofa, curling up beside him.

'We did meet him, but she didn't want to do the duet. She said she didn't want to sing with a wrinkly old man and she blamed me for us going to London.'

'So that's why she's slamming doors. She used to do a lot of that when she was young,' said Grandad, putting his arm round me.

'But something did happen today that was good, Grandad. She was able to remember some things.'

'Was she?' he said, his face lighting up. 'And what did she remember?'

'The sales. She remembered the both of us shopping in Selfridges in January and she remembered the lyrics of these songs by a singer she likes. I can't tell you how happy I was, Grandad. But she's still refusing to accept that she's my mum and I just can't bear it any more.'

Fourteen

'Your mum says she wants a new look,' said Grandad the next day.

Mum had already left to go to the hairdresser's when I woke up and Grandad was busy vacuuming. But what I wanted to know was whether any more of her memories had come back.

'She said she remembers when the two of us went on a day trip to Brighton,' said Grandad. 'It was before she had you and before she met your father. She said she remembered us eating jellied eels on the beach, which she spat out because she didn't like the taste, and she also said she remembers us buying souvenirs in a gift shop. But that was the only thing she was able to recall. She did complain about how untidy the house was, though, something she hasn't done since she left the hospital. You know how she used to fuss. So that's why I'm giving the carpet the once over. Your mum did some cleaning of her own before she left; she completely tidied up the kitchen.'

'It sounds like she's getting back to how she used to be. Maybe she's gone to the hairdresser's so she can have her hair back to how it was before she had the extensions put in.'

And maybe she'll start acting more like a mum as well, I thought.

'So are you all set for Layla's party tonight?' asked Grandad.

I nodded. 'I'm going to Layla's later for a final rehearsal. Afterwards me and my friends are all gonna get changed there then head straight to the party. I am looking forward to it but I'm a bit nervous about performing in front of all the people that are gonna be there, Grandad.'

'Oh, I'm sure you'll be fine, sweetheart. And what do I always say to you: shine, Izzy, shine. Just remember to smile and give it all you've got.'

After I'd made myself some breakfast – a toasted

ham sandwich with heaps of ketchup – I went and did my English and maths homework. I still had a couple of days before I had to hand it all in, but as Mum's memories were coming back I was suddenly worried that she might ask me if I'd done it – and I'd be able to honestly say that I had. It was a silly thing to worry about really, but if she'd started cleaning the house again, I didn't know what would come back to her next.

I put my new blouse and black shorts into my rucksack, along with my favourite lip gloss, my gold tassel necklace and Layla's present, which I'd put in a sparkly purple gift bag. I'd got her a Chase Dooley pencil case and notebook. I arrived at her house at the same time as Alice. Before either of us had rung the bell, Alice wanted to see what I'd got Layla, so I opened my rucksack to let her sneak a peek. Her present for Layla was wrapped in silver-coloured paper so I wasn't able to see it, but she said it contained a beauty pamper set along with a trinket box that looked like a giant cupcake.

Layla's mum answered the door and smiled cheerily as we went inside. 'I can't wait to see your performance tonight, girls,' she chirped. 'Layla's been singing that "Wings" song all morning. She's so excited about the party. Her dad's at the community centre right now putting up the decorations and making sure the place looks nice for this evening.'

Holly had already arrived when Alice and I went upstairs to Layla's room.

'Happy birthday!' Alice and I said in unison as we hugged our friend.

'Thank you so much,' said Layla, elated.

'And here's your present,' said Alice, giving Layla the parcel while I took mine out of my rucksack.

'I hope you don't mind, but I'm gonna open them later,' said Layla. 'I want to open all my presents at the same time.'

'So what did your parents get you?' I asked.

'Dunno yet. It's a surprise. But one present I do want, more than anything, is a tweet from Chase. I do know now that he's not gonna come to my party and it was silly of me to even think that he would, but I'm still hoping he'll send me a happy birthday tweet. I've sent him loads of tweets today asking him to do it.'

'Well, fingers crossed he'll tweet you back,' I replied.

'What are you wearing tonight, Layla?' asked Alice.

'This,' said Layla, grabbing a pair of black leggings that were hanging on her door and a gold sequinned top. 'What d'you think?'

I nodded approvingly. 'You're going to look amazing.'

We made space in Layla's room to practise our routine, moving her desk and other things to the side. Layla invited Alfie in to watch, but he decided he wanted to do some dancing of his own and was swinging his arms about as we went through our steps and sang the song. But none of us minded as our routine couldn't have gone any better and our harmonies were excellent.

'We're totally gonna blow everyone away tonight,' said Layla confidently. 'Our dance moves were brilliant, our vocals were brilliant. Who knows, maybe we've even got what it takes to be a real pop group.'

'Can I be in your group, Layla?' said Alfie very sweetly. 'I want to show everyone how good I can dance.'

'Sorry, little bro, but our group is for girls only,' she replied.

'That's not fair!' Alfie growled and stomped out of the room in a sulk.

Soon it was time for us to get ready for the party. Layla got us some popcorn and cans of Coke and turned up her stereo as we did each other's make-up. Alice did our hair. She gave me a wavy style using Layla's curling tongs and finished it off with heaps of hair spray that made us all cough.

'You look so much like Jade from Little Mix,' said Alice to me.

'And you look like you could be Leigh-Anne's little sister,' I said as Alice began styling her own hair.

'And do I look like Perrie?' said Holly, flipping her blonde tresses from side to side.

'Yeah, you do as it goes, and I think I definitely look like Jesy now,' said Layla as Alfie burst into the room. He was beside himself with excitement.

'It's here, Layla, the limo's here!'

'Yay!' said Holly, jumping up and down like it was the best news she'd ever heard.

My friends couldn't wait to get into the limo nor could Alfie who joined us with Layla's mum. The inside of the limo was dead plush with leather seats and a bar with two bottles of non-alcoholic cocktails that Layla's mum had made. She served them to us in fancy glasses and handed out canapés, which were smoked salmon and cream cheese on little pancakes she said were called blinis. Alfie kept playing with the electric windows, pressing the buttons to make them go up and down and waving out the window at people on the street.

'I feel like a celebrity,' said Layla.

'Me too,' said Holly, looking chuffed. 'I wish I had my own limo. I'd have it take me everywhere, even to school.'

I did enjoy being driven in the limo, but there was a pang in my chest as I remembered the last time I was in one, when Grandad and I were going to the hospital after Mum's accident.

As soon as the limo drew up outside the community centre, we all leaped out and made our way into the venue.

'How does it look, sweetie?' said Layla's dad walking up to greet us.

'It's perfect,' she beamed, wrapping her arms around him.

The place looked incredible. All round the room were pink and white drapes. A disco ball reflected multicoloured lights on to the floor. There was also a real stage; the chocolate fountain, which was huge; plus the candy floss machine; hot dog stall and photo booth Layla had mentioned. Master Slick was already there, setting up his mixing decks next to the stage. Layla was planning to greet her guests as they arrived, so went off to stand at the front entrance with her mum. Alice, Holly and me decided to go to the area Layla said was the 'chill-out zone' and sat down on a long pink velvet sofa adorned with cushions that had 'Layla's 13th' printed on them in gold writing. It was all very extravagant, but so very Layla.

'This party is already the best party I've ever been too,' said Holly. 'I'm definitely going to have cushions like this at my birthday party and a chocolate fountain and a candy floss machine. Do you think you'll have a party for your thirteenth, Izzy?'

'I'm not sure.'

My thirteenth birthday was still a few months away, just like Holly's, and I hadn't really thought about having a party. If I did have one, it certainly wouldn't be as flamboyant as Layla's, but then again I wouldn't mind having a chocolate fountain myself and a candy floss machine. Though to be honest, none of that sort of stuff really mattered to me any more, all I wanted was for my mum to get all her memories back.

'I really want to get Master Slick's autograph,' said Alice.

'So why don't you go and ask him for it?'

'I can't do that! I'm way too shy,' said Alice, sighing deeply.

I laughed. 'I thought it was me who was supposed to be the shy one. If you want, though, I'll come with you.'

'I will as well. It'll be cool to get his autograph,' said Holly.

'Oh. I've just realised . . . I don't have any paper,' said Alice.

'Then we'll just get him to sign these.' I picked up three napkins from a small table in front of us. We wandered over to him.

'Excuse me,' said Alice a little nervously, holding out the napkins to Master Slick. 'Could me and my friends have your autograph, please?'

'Sure. Do you have a pen?'

'Um . . .' She looked at me and Holly but we both shrugged.

'Actually I might have one,' said Master Slick, pulling a pen out of his back pocket and signing the napkins.

'See, that wasn't so difficult,' I said to Alice when we returned to the chill-out zone.

Soon the rest of Layla's guests started to arrive – her family and kids from school. Layla was still standing at the entrance greeting them all. Sam turned up with his friend Enzo and another boy called Parveen and as soon as I glimpsed him, my heart began to thud. But I refused to let my shyness stop me from going over to him.

'You look nice, Izzy,' he said, stepping away from his friends.

'Thanks,' I replied, my cheeks blushing.

'The music's good. I'd love to have Master Slick play at my party. I might just ask my parents if they can book him for my birthday next year.'

'I got his autograph earlier,' I said to Sam.

'He's doing autographs? Wicked. I think I'll ask him for one myself. So are you nervous about your performance?'

'I was, but I'm not any more 'cos we had another

practice today which went really well. I think everyone's going to really enjoy it.'

'It sounds like it's gonna be good. I look forward to seeing it. Anyway, I'll see you later, Izzy, and good luck with your performance,' said Sam and rejoined his friends.

'Soooo, what did he say?' said Holly, trying to pump me for information as she and Alice approached me.

'He wished me good luck for the performance,' I replied, smiling.

Suddenly the music stopped as the lights went out, plunging the room into darkness. Then a tapping sound came from the speakers.

'Right, peeps,' said Master Slick over the microphone. 'I think it's time we properly got this party started, don't you? So will you please give it up for the birthday girl herself, Layla!'

A white spotlight hit the floor as the music came back on and two guys breakdanced into the room. They were spinning on the floor, backflipping through the air and making their bodies move like robots; it was amazing. And right behind them was Layla, doing some awesome moves of her own. The whole room erupted into cheers.

'That was a terrific entrance,' I said to Layla when the dance routine had ended.

'Yeah, that was amazeballs,' Alice seconded.

'Why didn't you tell us you'd be having dancers with you?' said Holly, and I could tell from the look on her face she was already thinking about her own entrance for her birthday party.

'Because I wanted to surprise everyone,' said Layla, 'and I have been saying that I wanted my party to be one people never forget.'

As me and my friends went to dance, across the room I could see Sam looking my way. Alice had noticed him looking too.

'You should go over and dance with him,' she whispered.

'I don't know,' I dithered. 'What if I step on his foot or trip him up?'

'No, you won't,' she said. 'You're a great dancer, Izzy.'

I looked over again at Sam who'd gone back to chatting to his friends.

'Maybe I'll ask him after our performance,' I said, my stomach fizzing away at the thought of getting to dance with Sam.

Soon it was time for Layla to cut her cake. We

were all singing 'Happy Birthday' when suddenly Layla began to shriek.

'Aaaaah! I've got a tweet!' she said, cutting us off mid-song. 'Chase Dooley just sent me a happy birthday tweet. It says: "Have a great birthday, Layla. Love, Chase, kiss, kiss, kiss".'

She shrieked again and stuck out her phone to show us, everyone craning their necks to take a look.

'Let me see, let me see!' said Alfie, trying to grab her mobile, but Layla wasn't letting it go.

'He gave me kisses, three kisses!' she squealed, her eyes gleaming.

Layla's mum and dad gave her a cuddle.

'I told you he'd tweet you back,' said Layla's mum.

'Well done, Layla,' Alice called out to her.

'You're so lucky, Layla,' said a girl in our year called Becky Scanlan, but her face looked dead jealous. 'I wish I had a tweet from a celebrity,' I heard her say to another girl.

Layla's dad cleared his throat very loudly to quieten us all down.

'Right, I think we should start the song again,' he said.

So we all sang 'Happy Birthday' for a second time and took photos on our phones as Layla blew out the candles on her cake.

'Layla, your mum and I would like to give you your present now,' said Layla's dad as the auntie who'd been guarding Layla's presents carried over a gold envelope.

Layla gasped as she tore it open. 'Little Mix tickets!' She hugged both her parents, her face brimming with happiness.

'We know how much you wanted to see them in concert,' said Layla's dad. 'There are also four more tickets, one for your mum and another three for you to take your friends.'

Layla looked over at me, Holly and Alice, and waved the tickets which made us jump about giddily.

'I can't wait for us to go and see Little Mix,' said Layla when we were getting some food.

'I can't wait either, and I just know the concert's going to be amazing,' I replied cheerfully.

'And it's so great that you got a tweet from Chase,' said Holly.

'I know, I can't believe it,' Layla trilled.

A short while later it was time for our

performance, the four of us making our way to the side of the stage as we waited for Master Slick to introduce us.

'Girls, you all look fabulous, so let's just go out there and rock this place!' said Layla.

'Yeah, let's rock!' we all said high-fiving each other.

'We now have a very special performance for you, everyone.' Master Slick's voice poured through the speakers. 'Please put your hands together and make some noise for Layla, Izzy, Alice and Holly!'

We sprinted onto the stage to a rapturous applause, then picked up our microphones and took our places. Then when the music started, we fired straight into our routine. And from the second we began to sing I was truly having the time of my life. Plus I didn't feel the least bit nervous. In fact, it felt wonderful performing in front of everyone and I felt like I already was a pop star.

Then suddenly it was as if everything froze – I spotted a familiar face among the crowd. I hadn't noticed her coming in, but she was swiftly making her way to the front, pushing her way through. It was Mum, but she didn't look like Mum. Her hair was short again, but it was dyed green, bright green.

And not only that, but she was wearing the jean shorts I'd bought in London and my new top that had 'Gonna Be Famous' written across it, her belly poking out underneath. And there was something glinting under her lower lip. It was a stud. She'd had her face pierced!

Fifteen

I could see some kids staring at Mum and I was hoping with all my might that they didn't realise she was my mum. But then those same kids and lots more began to stare at me and for a moment I feared that they'd guessed who she was.

'Izzy, what are you doing?' hissed Layla, snapping me out of my haze and making me realise that what I'd been doing was nothing at all. I'd stopped singing and dancing; that's why everyone was staring. I quickly tried to copy the dance steps that the others were doing but it was pointless, I couldn't keep up, plus I'd forgotten the lyrics to the song.

'You've ruined the routine, Izzy. You're ruined it!' yelled Layla, dropping her microphone, tears spurting from her eyes. She stormed off the stage along with Holly and Alice who also looked very cross. The music was halted, and except for a few mutterings here and there the room was silent. Very slowly I came down from the stage. I felt completely stupid.

'What happened out there, Izzy?' said Mum, rushing up.

But I just rolled my eyes at her. 'Why have you dyed your hair green and your face... you've got a stud in your face!'

'I fancied a new look,' she replied. 'Do you like it?'

'No! You look awful and I can't believe that you're wearing my clothes again.'

I'd never felt more embarrassed, especially as there were kids staring at the two of us. I just hoped Sam wasn't looking. I'd already embarrassed myself once tonight and I certainly didn't need my mum humiliating me again.

'And why are you even here?' I barked. 'This is a teenager's party. You shouldn't be here.'

'I've always liked a good party and this one seems fun,' she replied, then launched into these dippy dance moves which might've looked cool in the nineties, but right now were total cringe.

If only the ground would swallow me up, I thought, so I could escape the embarrassment.

'Stop it, Rio. Everyone's looking at us,' I shouted at her as Layla came over with Holly and Alice. She wasn't crying any more, but her face was red and puffy.

'Why did you just stop like that, Iz? Did you forget the routine, or something?' she said, her voice all interrogative. Her lips were pursed in an angry pout.

I chewed my lip as I tried to think of what to say.

'You know how hard we worked to get the routine right so I can't understand why you just stopped like that. Did you get stage fright, was that it?'

Then she noticed my mum.

'Gosh,' Layla muttered, her eyes widening. 'Miss Silva. Hi. Sorry, I didn't recognise you.'

She blinked at Mum rapidly. So did Holly and Alice.

'Someone should've told her mum that it wasn't a fancy-dress party,' I suddenly heard someone say. The voice sounded like Becky Scanlan's, which alarmed me 'cos I always thought Becky was nice.

'Is that really her mother?' I heard another voice say in a catty tone.

I turned round to see who it was, but there were so many kids staring at us that it was hard to tell who'd said it.

'I think it *is* her mum,' I heard a third voice sneer, followed by laughter. 'She looks like a right weirdo.'

That was it! I couldn't listen to any more.

'If you want to know why my mum looks the way she does, it's because she has amnesia. She thinks she's fourteen,' I screeched, looking at all their faces. Then I ran as fast as I could right out of the community centre and all the way down to the end of the road before stopping, gasping for breath and crying my eyes out.

'Izzy.' I could hear my mum's voice in the distance.

It took her a while to catch up; she couldn't run as fast.

'Why did you tell everyone I had amnesia?' she said when she eventually caught up with me.

'Because they were staring at you, that's why. You look like a clown with that stupid green hair and my clothes make you look like mutton dressed as lamb.'

'But I like these clothes,' said Mum, 'and my new hair.'

'But they're *my* clothes. Not yours. Mine,' I said as more tears poured down my cheeks. 'I'm sick of you, Mum, I really am.'

But before she could complain about me calling her 'Mum' again, I sped off, this time all the way home. I didn't look back once.

'Has the party ended already? I thought Layla's mum was going to drop you back at ten,' said Grandad when I got in, but then he saw my tears. 'Oh dear, it looks like someone needs a hug and a cup of Grandad's special hot chocolate.'

'Mum showed up at the party,' I said to him. 'She's dyed her hair green and she's got a piercing under her lip; plus she was wearing the clothes I bought in London. She really embarrassed me, Grandad. And I didn't even get the chance to dance with—'

I thought of Sam. I never got the chance to ask him if he'd like to dance with me. Grandad went off to make the hot chocolate and when he came back I couldn't wait to drink it. It felt so soothing and warm.

'Did you know Mum was going to come to the party?'

'No, not at all,' he said. 'I was watching the news when she came home earlier, but she went straight upstairs then right back out again. I didn't see her. She also left her phone behind so I couldn't call her to find out where she was heading.'

'I just don't get why she's acting like this, Grandad. It's like she's become a different person,' I murmured in Portuguese.

'It's like she's rebelling again, just like she did when she was a teenager,' said Grandad. 'Sometimes I really don't know how I should be treating her. Should I treat her like the teenager she thinks she is or the adult that she really is?'

I shrugged my shoulders.

'I suppose I should really be treating her like an adult, perhaps that would help her to adjust,' said Grandad. 'Do you remember when I told you on the day of the wedding how your mum once dyed her hair blue?'

I nodded feebly.

'She was fifteen years old and was a right little madam, I can tell you, always getting into trouble at school. I can't tell you the number of times her headteacher would summon me up there because she'd skipped some lesson or another. Then there was her constant sneaking out to go to parties, just like tonight, which makes me think that perhaps she's trying to get in touch with all of that again. She keeps saying she doesn't want to be an adult; so she goes and does the opposite – behaves like a rebellious teenager.'

'I don't think she ever wanted me to know about that rebellious side to her,' I said to him. 'Before her accident, Mum was always making out that she a goody two-shoes but I guess the Mum I'm seeing now is the Mum you knew as a teenager.'

'I used to think she went off the rails when she was young because of her mother dying,' said Grandad. 'I used to see it as Rio's way of coming to terms with the fact that her mother was no longer around. But she did change when she had you, Izzy. She became a really sensible young woman, and all that partying she used to do, she gave it all up to concentrate on being the best mum she could for you.'

'I just wish so much that her accident had never happened. I hate it that Malcolm's not here any more. I miss him, Grandad.'

'The place certainly isn't the same without him,' Grandad replied.

I called Layla's mobile to see if Mum had returned to the party, but she told me that she hadn't. She also apologised for having a go at me, but wanted to know why I didn't tell her that my mum had been suffering from amnesia.

'I suppose I was worried what you'd say and I didn't want everyone feeling sorry for me,' I admitted.

'The thing is, Izzy, by not telling me it meant I couldn't be there for you like a best friend should,' said Layla gently.

Two hours went by but Mum still hadn't come home and it was now half past ten.

'Maybe you should think about getting some sleep, Izzy. I'll wait up for your mum,' said Grandad in Portuguese.

'Actually, I'd like to wait up for her if that's OK. It's not as if I've got school tomorrow or anything.'

'But she's probably just somewhere having a coffee. I'm sure she'll be home soon,' he said.

But he let me stay up and soon an hour passed then another one and I was starting to get very worried. I asked Grandad if he thought we should call the police and tell them Mum was missing.

'No, I don't think that'll be necessary,' he responded. 'She's only been gone a few hours so let's not panic just yet.'

We got through a few more cups of hot chocolate as we continued to wait. We watched an old episode of this game show called *Bullseye* which Grandad said was a very popular show in the eighties but I thought the programme was pretty dire. And the prizes that a couple won at the end were so naff. OK, they did win a holiday to Tenerife but they also won a crummy old clock and a rubbish-looking camera, which wasn't even a digital one. Once the show had ended Grandad turned over the channel to a film. We were about ten minutes into it when it dawned on us that it was actually a horror film. A half-man, half-monster terrified the life out of us as it burst onto the screen and ripped a woman's head off, blood splattering everywhere. And suddenly I began to fret even more.

What if Mum's been kidnapped by a psychopath? What if we never see her again?

I got up and ran outside, my eyes scouring the dark deserted street.

'Come back inside, Izzy, it's late,' called Grandad from the doorway.

'But where is she, Grandad? Why hasn't she come home yet?' I said, looking at him desperately before trudging back inside.

I looked at my mobile. I had two new texts from Alice and three from Holly. But right now I wasn't in the mood to reply to them. I was only concerned about Mum.

'Do you think Mum might be in danger, that someone is holding her against her will?' I asked Grandad.

'It's that film that's got that idea into your head. I wish I'd never changed the channel,' said Grandad. 'No, Izzy, I don't think anyone is holding your mother against her will.'

'Well, do you think she might've got lost, then? She doesn't remember the whole town. Or what if she's collapsed, Grandad? She might be all on her own with no one to call an ambulance.'

'Please try not to worry, Izzy, but let's just say if she's not back in two hours' time, we'll call the police,' said Grandad in a calm fashion. 'I tell you what, why don't we play a game of Scrabble, help take our mind off things?'

So that's what we did, we played some Scrabble and for once I actually managed to beat my grandad and win the game, although a part of me couldn't help thinking that maybe he allowed me to win as a way of trying to cheer me up. Afterwards we watched some more telly, a cookery reality show that had a chef in it that seemed to spend most of his time shouting at all the wannabe chefs he was supposed to be training. Just as it was about to end we heard the sound of keys in the door. It was Mum.

'Where have you been? We were really worried about you,' I said to her, feeling cross.

'I went for a walk,' she mumbled.

'A walk, at two o'clock at night,' said Grandad, no longer calm but very, very angry. 'Why, Rio?'

'I needed to have a think, Dad,' she said in Portuguese.

'A think? What about?' said Grandad.

Mum sighed. 'Just . . . things.'

'But anything could've happened to you, Rio,' said Grandad. 'You have amnesia, which makes you vulnerable. And what have you done to yourself? Your hair looks atrocious,' he remarked, sounding like he does when he tells me off.

But Mum just shrugged her shoulders, her eyes downcast.

'You do know you left your mobile behind,' said Grandad and held up Mum's phone.

'I'm not used to carrying a phone around. Look, I just want to go up to bed. I'm feeling really tired so night, Dad, night, Izzy,' she said and sloped out of the room.

'Well, at least she's back,' said Grandad, sitting back down on the sofa, 'and now I think it's time for your bedtime too, sweetheart.'

I went up to my room, but I didn't go to sleep straightaway. I decided to write my mum a letter. I wanted to tell her how I felt and how much I missed the old her. I thought a letter would have more impact than me simply saying it to her.

Dear Mum,

I know there are a lot of things you can't remember, but I just want you to know that you're the best mum anyone could have. You've always been there for me, giving me advice and putting a smile on my face whenever I've been down. When you had your accident I really thought I was going to lose you. I was so scared, Mum. But when you came out of the coma, I was ever so happy. I know you don't like me calling you 'Mum' right now, but I really do miss being able to call you that. It makes me so sad that I can't. I know you're finding it difficult trying to get used to being a mum, but I can help you if you let me. I'm sorry that I said I was sick of you when I ran off from Layla's party. I didn't mean it, honest. But I didn't like seeing you in my clothes or with green hair. You might not know it but you're really different to how you used to be and I really miss the old you. When your amnesia goes away I hope you'll go back to being the mum I love so much.

Yours,
Izzy x

Later that night, I snuck into Mum's room as she slept and put the letter on her bedside table.

Sixteen

When I woke up on Sunday morning my first thought was whether Mum had read my letter. She was in the kitchen with Grandad when I went downstairs, and they were both filling a picnic basket.

'What's going on?' I asked.

'And a very good morning to you too, Izzy,' said Grandad.

'Sorry,' I apologised. 'Why have you got that basket out?'

'Because we're going on a picnic this afternoon,' said Mum. She smiled, but I couldn't tell from her expression if she'd read the letter or not. It was still strange seeing her with green hair, but for once she was wearing her own clothes, a pair of beige linen trousers and a white sleeveless shirt; and I noticed she'd taken out the stud from under her lip.

'It's a fine day outside so I thought a picnic would be a nice treat for all of us,' said Grandad.

'We've been making sandwiches,' said Mum. 'Ham and pickle, and cheese and tomato; that last one's your favourite, right?'

'Did you remember that?' I said, suddenly feeling excited that maybe she'd remembered some more things.

'Actually, I told her,' said Grandad. 'We've also put in some crisps, some chicken drumsticks and that box of carrot cake slices I bought the other day.'

The park was busy with people having picnics and lying in the sun enjoying the warmth. Me, Mum and Grandad found a spot under an oak tree to lay out our picnic.

'Do you remember this park?' I asked Mum as she munched on some crisps. 'We used to come here all the time when I was little. We'd come to feed the ducks or you'd take me to the playground.'

'I only remember it from when I was young,' she replied. 'Not much has changed, though. It looks exactly as it did when Rhona and I would come here to bunk off school. But parks are something that never change, aren't they?'

'I guess not,' said Grandad. He sighed. 'I still can't believe you dyed your hair green, Rio.'

'I'm surprised Kye didn't recommend another colour to you,' I added.

'I didn't see Kye. I went to a different hair-dresser's, but, trust me, I won't be going back,' said Mum. 'Anyway it's not permanent, it'll come out after a few washes.'

'I told Izzy it was as if you'd begun rebelling again just like you did when you were a teenager,' said Grandad.

'And yesterday I still wanted to be that teenager,' said Mum.

'So does that mean you accept that you're an adult now?' I said, looking at Mum hopefully.

'If you're trying to suss out whether I read your letter or not, well, I did as it happens,' she said.

'What letter?' asked Grandad.

'Izzy wrote a letter to me last night, a very deep letter. She'd like me to be how I was before my amnesia,' Mum said to him.

'I wasn't trying to be horrible or anything. I care about you,' I said.

'I know,' Mum nodded. 'Look, I'm sorry about turning up at your friend's party and embarrassing you the way I did. I've been behaving really crazily. I guess it's just because I couldn't accept that I was a mum with responsibilities. I wanted to be the teenager who sang songs with her friends in the playground and could never get her homework in on time.'

'Just like me, but I did finish the homework I had this week,' I told her.

'Yesterday I still wanted to be the fourteen-year-old I am in my head,' said Mum.

'And what about today?' I asked her.

'Well, I've accepted that I'm not fourteen any more and that I have amnesia. I also know that I'm a grown-up woman with a daughter.'

She smiled at me.

'And my memories are coming back now. Slowly, but they're coming back.'

'Was there something else that you remembered?' I asked.

'Yes, there was actually, just this morning when I woke up. I remembered you as a baby, Izzy. I was rocking you to sleep and I was singing a song to you – "What A Wonderful World".'

'That's your favourite song,' said Grandad.

Mum smiled again.

'I also remembered when you walked for the first time. I'd turned round to pick something up, it might have been a toy or something else, but when I turned back, you were standing up all by yourself. You walked a few steps towards me and I picked you up and gave you a massive cuddle. And as those memories were coming back to me, I had such a feeling of love come over me. I remembered how much I love you, Izzy, and how much you mean to me.'

'And you mean a lot to me too, Mum – sorry, Rio,' I said, my voice trailing off.

'No, it's OK, Izzy. You can call me Mum. Because that's what I am and that's what I'm going to try to be again,' she said as she reached out and took my hand in hers.

* * *

I was over the moon that Mum had finally accepted that she was my mum and that some more of her memories had come back. After the picnic, the three of us took another trip around the town to see if a few of the local landmarks could jog more of Mum's memories. We went back to the art gallery on the high street and she remembered an exhibition that the two of us went to which was showcasing pictures that had different coloured dots in the middle of a white canvas. At the time both Mum and I thought the pictures were daft and had said we could do pictures like that ourselves. We were also shocked that each of the pictures cost over a thousand pounds. Mum remembered that and she remembered when she used to take me to a drop-in story-time session at the library where we went to next. Afterwards we went to the ice-skating rink which was fun. Both Mum and me did some skating, but as Grandad can't skate he sat and read a newspaper instead. When we came off the ice, Mum had some more thrilling news. She'd remembered something else.

'I remember skating here with Malcolm. It was our second date and I remember how happy I felt with him.'

'That's brilliant, Mum,' I said, feeling really pleased, and I knew Malcolm would be pleased too when I told him.

When we got home I couldn't wait to call Malcolm and let him know what Mum had remembered, but first I had to reply to all the texts Alice and Holly had been sending me. They were apologising for being mean to me at the party. I texted them back to say that all was forgiven and as soon as I sent my text to Holly she immediately called my phone.

'So is it true your mum thinks she's fourteen?' she asked.

'Well, yes, but actually we had a really good day today,' I told her. 'She accepts that she's an adult now and she knows she has amnesia, but the great thing is her memories are coming back. I really hope this means that her amnesia is finally going away.'

When I called Malcolm to tell him that Mum had remembered how she felt about him, he literally sobbed with happiness.

'Now that her memories are coming back, it means you can come home, Malcolm,' I chirped.

But then he sounded hesitant.

‘It’s probably still too early for me to come back if the only thing she can remember about our relationship is when we went to the ice rink. I think it’s probably better I wait until she’s remembered some other things about us.’

‘She will remember, Malcolm, so why don’t you just come over tomorrow and see us? Or even tonight,’ I added.

‘You know I’d love that more than anything, Izzy. But I wouldn’t want to upset Rio. She needs to be completely ready to see me.’

I was so disappointed, I was hoping for everything to get back to normal as soon as possible, but I guessed I’d just have to be patient. I really wanted Malcolm and Mum back together. But I realised he was right; Mum needed a bit more time.

As a new week began, even more of Mum’s memories started to come back. She remembered when she used to take me swimming and when I used to play my old recorder around the house just to annoy her. And she was able to recall the time when we went to the funfair and her candy floss blew away in the wind. She remembered the nativity play I was in at primary school, and the first time I showed her the picture I painted of the two of us at Bristol Zoo. And she said she remembered my dad and the sadness she felt when he left us.

We all found it so strange the way her memories were coming back in dribs and drabs, but when Mum spoke to her therapist about it, she reassured her that it was completely normal. I couldn't work out what was triggering these memories, but I kept showing her photos and telling her about special moments in her life. We also played lots of music that we liked – especially the stuff she and Malcolm loved to dance to. I was determined to get Mum to remember everything about Malcolm soon.

Any time she remembered something new, I'd call Malcolm to tell him. But he was still reluctant to see Mum, as most of those memories weren't about him. I also told my friends what my mum had remembered – they were all very happy for me.

On Tuesday afternoon before the start of French, Sam came up to my desk. He didn't mention the party, which was a relief, but he did tell me about his uncle again.

'When my uncle had his bike accident, Izzy, he forgot a couple of things,' he started telling me. 'He couldn't remember when he taught me all there was to know about motorbikes and when I used to help him wash his bike, or when we'd go to football matches, or go camping with my brother. It made me quite sad that he'd forgotten all that stuff. When he first came out of his coma, he couldn't even remember my name. But the amnesia didn't last long. Anyway, I just thought I'd tell you that because I kind of understand what you're going through.'

'Thanks, Sam.' I smiled and he gave me the cutest smile back.

'I see a new relationship starting by the end of term,' whispered Layla, who was sitting next to me.

But for once I didn't roll my eyes at her. Who knew what would happen between me and Sam. One thing I did know was that I was no longer shy when it came to speaking to him – I considered him a friend, and that was enough for me just now.

As that week went by, more of Mum's memories came back, and on the Friday night Mum had me grinning from ear to ear with one particular memory. She, me and Grandad were eating dinner when she just came out with it.

'I remember when Malcolm proposed to me,' she said. 'I remember the picnic we had, and the little dog trying to steal our food. I remember the ring and how excited I felt about becoming his wife.'

I couldn't stop smiling.

Seventeen

A couple of weeks later, nearly all of Mum's memories had returned. It was like a miracle. She'd been working really hard with the therapist from the hospital, who gave her more tips and exercises to help her memories return more quickly.

Mum could now remember her job as a press officer at the council and all her colleagues. She could remember when she, me and Malcolm moved into our house and all the holidays we'd gone on. She remembered the recipe for her Thai green curry and a recipe for a beef stew she sometimes makes. She also remembered when my first baby tooth fell out, the one I put in the scrapbook, and remembered putting a fifty-pence piece under my pillow and telling me it was the tooth fairy who'd put it there. And she could now remember her wedding day and the accident. She said that she'd suddenly lost her footing and fallen, and then everything went black.

It was so lovely to have my mum back and it was strange to see it happening gradually. As her memories came back, so did her all her mum character traits – she was back to being Miss Perfect and keeping everything tidy. And it was funny, now she was getting back to herself, there was a little part of me that felt quite relieved knowing that when she was my age, she wasn't perfect and good at everything either. If anything, it made me feel closer to her.

I knew Mum's feelings for Malcolm had returned because I kept catching her looking at photos of them together on her phone and in the scrapbook. And one night when Grandad and I had gone to bed, Mum stayed up to watch the DVD of their engagement party. I'd snuck down and she was staring at the TV screen intently, a soppy smile on her face. And it was then when I decided that I had to do something to get her and Malcolm back together.

I came up with a plan: I'd text Malcolm from Mum's phone, pretending to be her, and invite him to come over for a Thai green curry dinner on Tuesday evening. Then on Tuesday afternoon, when I got in from school, I'd tell Mum that I fancied having Thai green curry for dinner and ask her to make it.

Tuesday came and I put the plan into action. Malcolm agreed to come over and Mum agreed to make the curry. Mum had no idea Malcolm was coming, and neither did Grandad, so when there was a knock at the door at six p.m., they both looked up in surprise.

'I'll get it,' I said.

Malcolm was holding a bunch of flowers. He was wearing a proper shirt and tie, and looked very nervous. As I led him through to the kitchen both Mum and Grandad couldn't believe their eyes.

'Malcolm,' Mum gasped.

'Hello, Rio,' he said shyly. 'It's really good to see you. Thanks for inviting me over for dinner.'

'Erm, I didn't—'

'It was me, Malcolm, I invited you,' I said swiftly. 'I sent the text on Mum's phone. She didn't know you were coming. But the reason why I wanted you to come tonight is because I want you and Mum to talk. I know how much you love my mum, Malcolm, and I know, Mum, that you now remember how much you love Malcolm.'

Both Mum and Malcolm began to blush.

'By the way, these are for you,' said Malcolm, handing the flowers to Mum.

'They're daisies, my favourite,' she said, setting them down on the table.

'You remember.' Malcolm smiled.

'I certainly do,' said Mum, but then, all of a sudden, she dashed out the kitchen and went upstairs. I was scared she might've gone off in a huff because she didn't want Malcolm here.

'She's probably just popped to the toilet,' I quickly said to him, trying to keep my voice steady and cool, but my heart thumped with worry.

It was an awkward few minutes as we waited for Mum to come back down; me, Malcolm and Grandad, sitting tensely in the living room. But when she did, she had a very cheery smile on her face. She'd also changed into the blue Topshop dress she'd bought in London. She looked lovely.

'I thought I'd change seeing as we have a guest,' she said and smiled at Malcolm. 'Right, I'll just go and get the dinner.'

'Oh, Izzy and I will see to that,' said Grandad, beckoning to me. 'You sit down and chat to Malcolm.'

I joined Grandad in the kitchen to serve up the dinner, but we took our time so that Mum and Malcolm could talk in private.

'I know she probably won't ask him to come back straightaway, but I'm hoping that they'll start going out again,' I said to Grandad.

When we went back to the living room to tell Mum and Malcolm the food was ready, they were in deep conversation.

'I was just telling Rio about the first time I met you, Julius, and the look you gave me when you saw what was written on my T-shirt,' said Malcolm.

'Oh yes, it was the one that said "Keep Calm and Carry on Burping", wasn't it?' said Grandad, cracking up with laughter. 'I remember thinking to myself: my Rio can't possibly be serious about this man.'

'I don't remember that day. But I do remember when we went to London for a romantic weekend. We visited an art gallery that had a big exhibition on,' said Mum. 'You were wearing a T-shirt that said "Can I help?" and I remember going to the toilet, and when I got back you were surrounded by tourists who thought you worked at the gallery. You really do have the wackiest but most brilliant T-shirts, Malcolm.'

'Thanks,' said Malcolm, gazing at Mum affectionately. 'I remember that day as well. I don't think I've worn that T-shirt since. But I really enjoyed the weekend, it was very special.'

As we ate dinner I was bubbling with excitement – the evening was going so well! It was clear Mum and Malcolm were enjoying being in each other's company – even if they were being a bit formal with each other.

'I've really missed you, Rio,' said Malcolm, after we'd eaten and had settled back down in the living room.

'You really care about me, don't you?' said Mum, looking at him. 'I said some terrible things to you in the hospital, but I'd like it if we could put it all behind us if that's OK,' she continued. 'I'm glad you're here and I certainly don't want this to be the last time we have dinner so maybe we could go out for a meal next time?'

'Yeah, I'd really like that,' said Malcolm, looking pleased.

'Then it's a date,' said Mum.

'So, what's for dessert?' asked Grandad.

Mum put her hand over her mouth. 'Oops, we don't have anything!'

'Really, nothing at all?' said Grandad.

'We do have some strawberries, Mum, in the fridge. And cream,' I said.

Malcolm cleared his throat. 'Now I know I'm not the best cook, but if you don't mind, I'd like to get this. Strawberries and cream is fairly easy to make, although I might just experiment with a few chopped peanuts over it if you have any,' he said, grinning.

'I'm sure we have some peanuts somewhere.' Mum smiled as she got up from the sofa. 'I'll help you find them.'

'Your mum and Malcolm are getting on rather nicely, don't you think?' said Grandad after they'd gone to the kitchen. 'It's just like old times.'

'And the good thing is, I still have my bridesmaid's dress,' I said, raising my eyebrows.

'And I still have my suit. Fingers crossed, we'll get another chance to wear them.'

'Fingers crossed,' I said, smiling. 'Hopefully we'll get to wear them again very, very soon.'

About the Author

Born and raised in London, where she still lives today, Ellie Daines always aspired to one day become an author, and as a child she spent much of her spare time writing short stories. At university, Ellie studied journalism and then later worked in online marketing for several companies. Her first book, *Lolly Luck*, was published by Andersen Press.

To find out more about Ellie Daines visit: www.elliedaines.com

Lolly Luck

ELLIE DAINES

Lolly is Lolly Luck by name, lucky by nature. She always wins magazine competitions, on scratch cards and any game you can think of. But when Lolly's dad loses his job and then the family home, Lolly's luck starts to change. And when she overhears her parents arguing, she learns a secret that will change her life forever.

'Great stuff. Readers will be cheering Lolly every step of the way' *Ally Kennen*

9781849393966 £5.99

WINNER OF THE GUARDIAN CHILDREN'S FICTION PRIZE AND SHORTLISTED FOR THE CARNEGIE MEDAL

When Georges moves into a new apartment block he meets Safer, a twelve-year-old self-appointed spy. Soon Georges has become his spy recruit. His first assignment? To track the mysterious Mr X, who lives in the flat upstairs. But as Safer becomes more demanding, Georges starts to wonder: what is a game and what is a lie? How far is too far to go for your only friend?

'A joy to read' *Independent*

'Rebecca Stead makes writing this well look easy' *Philip Ardagh, Guardian*

9781849395427 £6.99 Paperback

The Boy on the Porch

SHARON CREECH

When John and Marta found the boy on the porch, they were curious, naturally, as to why he was there – and they hadn't expected him to stay, not at first, but he did stay, day after day, until it seemed as if he belonged.

As the couple's connection to mysterious boy grows, the three of them blossom into an unlikely family. But where has he come from and to whom does he belong?

In this moving story, Carnegie Medal winner Sharon Creech poignantly reminds us of the surprising relationships that can bloom when generosity and unconditional love prevail.

9781783440863 £6.99

Abela

BERLIE DOHERTY

Two girls.

Abela lives in an African village and has lost everything. What will be her fate as an illegal immigrant? Will she find a family in time?

'I don't want a sister or brother,' thinks Rosa in England. Could these two girls ever become sisters?

Abela is the powerful and moving story of a true heroine who overcomes great hardship. Double Carnegie-winning author Berlie Doherty writing at her very best.

Shortlisted for the Manchester Book Award, the Coventry Inspiration Book Award 2009 and The Blue Peter Book Awards.

'Excellent . . . what could be an unbearably sad tale is made compulsively readable by a writer of grace and skill.' *Independent*

HBK 9781842706893 £10.99
PBK 9781842707258 £5.99

Run Rabbit Run

BARBARA MITCHELHILL

When Lizzie's dad refuses to fight in the Second World War, the police come looking to arrest him. Desperate to stay together, Lizzie and her brother Freddie go on the run with him, hiding from the police in idyllic Whiteway. But when their past catches up with them, they're forced to leave and it becomes more and more difficult to stay together as a family. Will they be able to? And will they ever find a place, like Whiteway, where they will be safe again?

Nominated for the Carnegie Medal

'A well-told story showing that bravery comes in many guises.'
Carousel

9781849392495 £6.99